SO-AAB-599

BIG DREAMS

A GRAPHIC NOVEL

by Brooke Vitale

An Imprint of

SCHOLASTIC

All rights reserved. Published by Graphix, an imprint of Scholastic Inc.,
Publishers since 1920. SCHOLASTIC, GRAPHIX, and associated logos are trademarks
and/or registered trademarks of Scholastic Inc.

ISBN 978-1-338-74329-6

10 9 8 7 6 5 4 3 2 1   21 22 23 24 25

Printed in the U.S.A. 40

First edition, September 2021
Written by Brooke Vitale
Illustrated by Artful Doodlers, Ltd.
Book design by Jeff Shake

FIRST DAY
OF SCHOOL

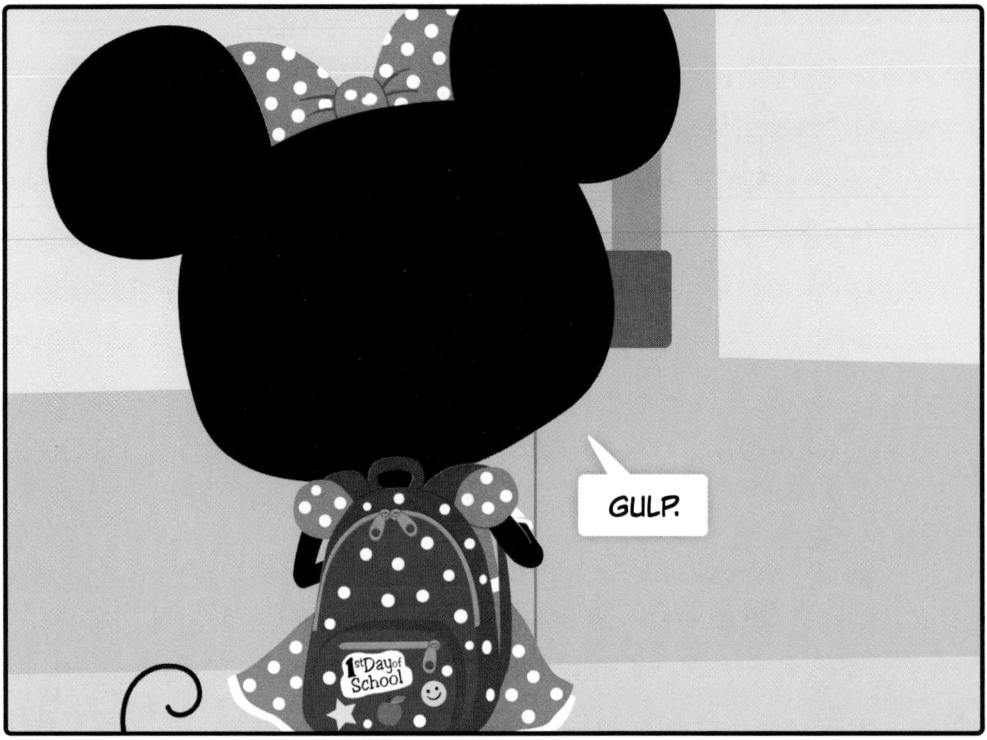
1st Day of School
GULP.

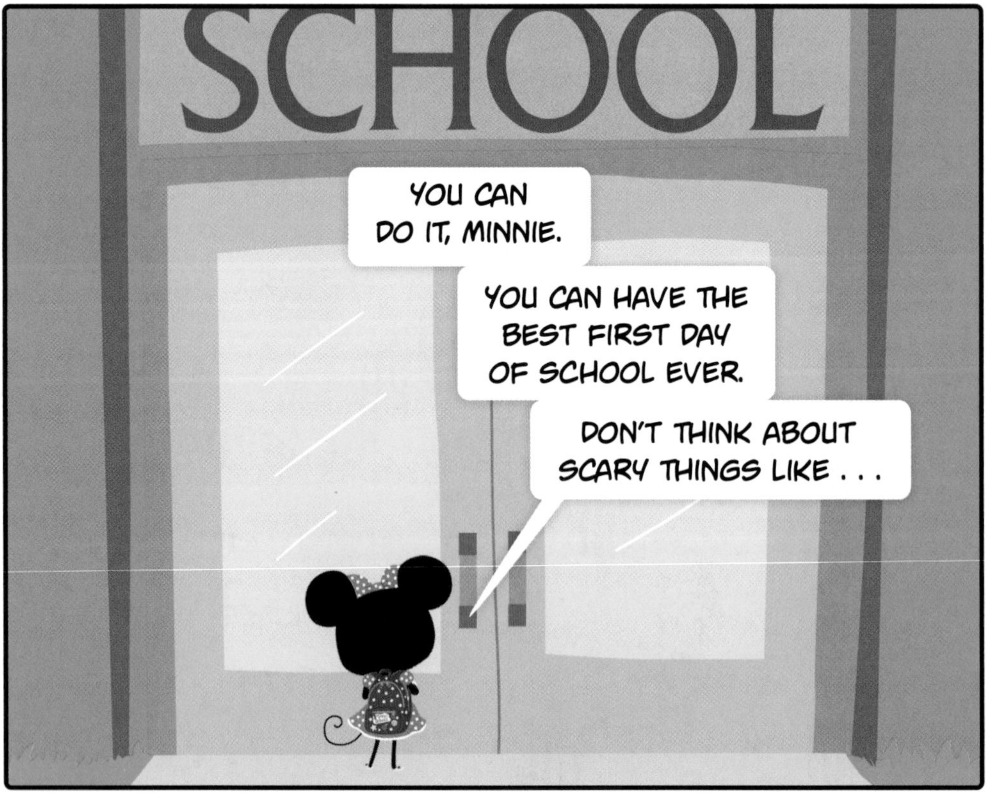
SCHOOL
YOU CAN DO IT, MINNIE.
YOU CAN HAVE THE BEST FIRST DAY OF SCHOOL EVER.
DON'T THINK ABOUT SCARY THINGS LIKE . . .

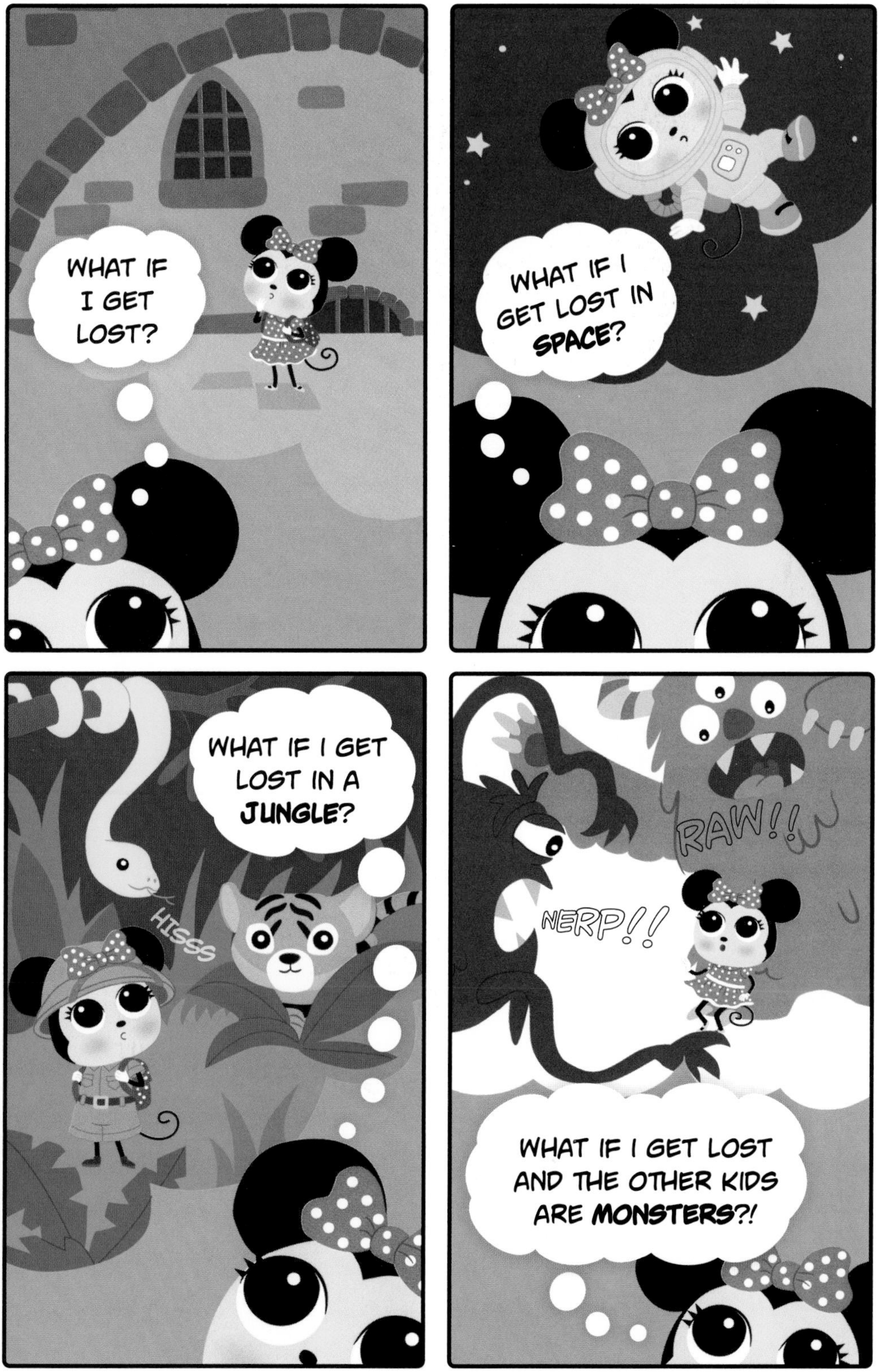
WHAT IF I GET LOST?
WHAT IF I GET LOST IN SPACE?
WHAT IF I GET LOST IN A JUNGLE?
HISSS
RAW!!
NERP!!
WHAT IF I GET LOST AND THE OTHER KIDS ARE MONSTERS?!

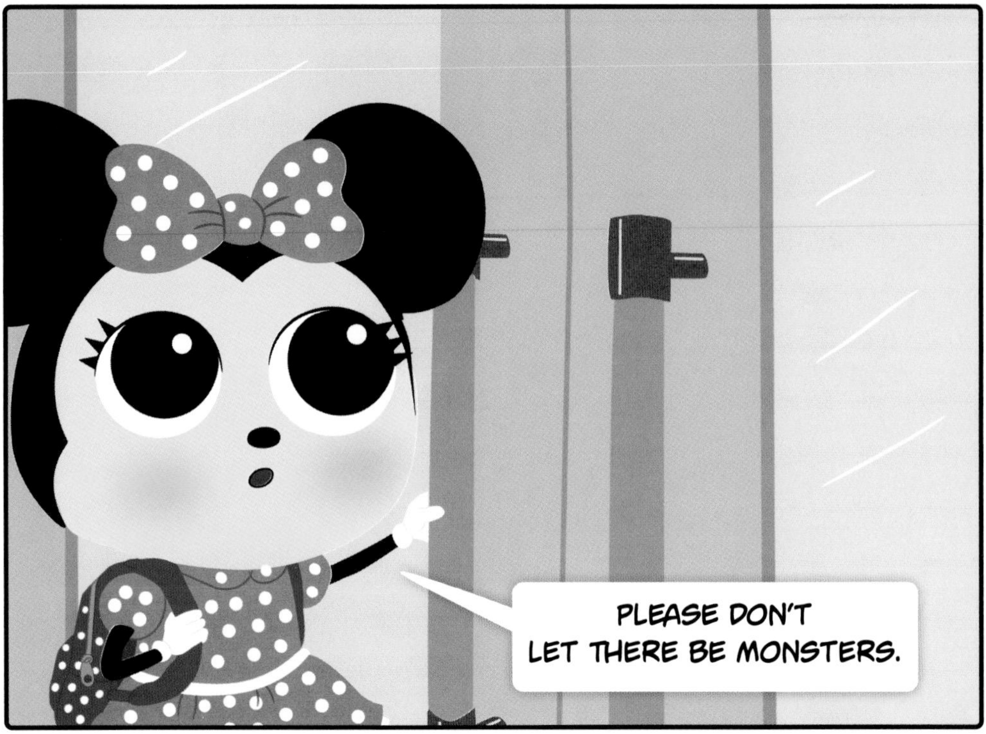
PLEASE DON'T
LET THERE BE MONSTERS.

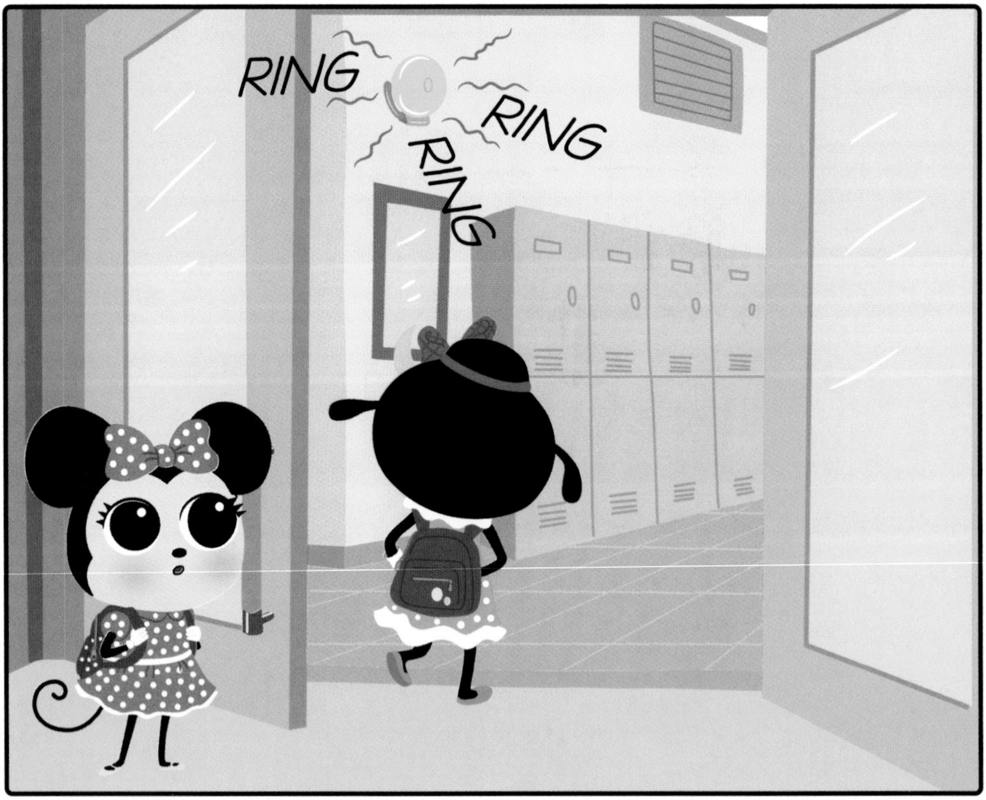
RING
RING
RING

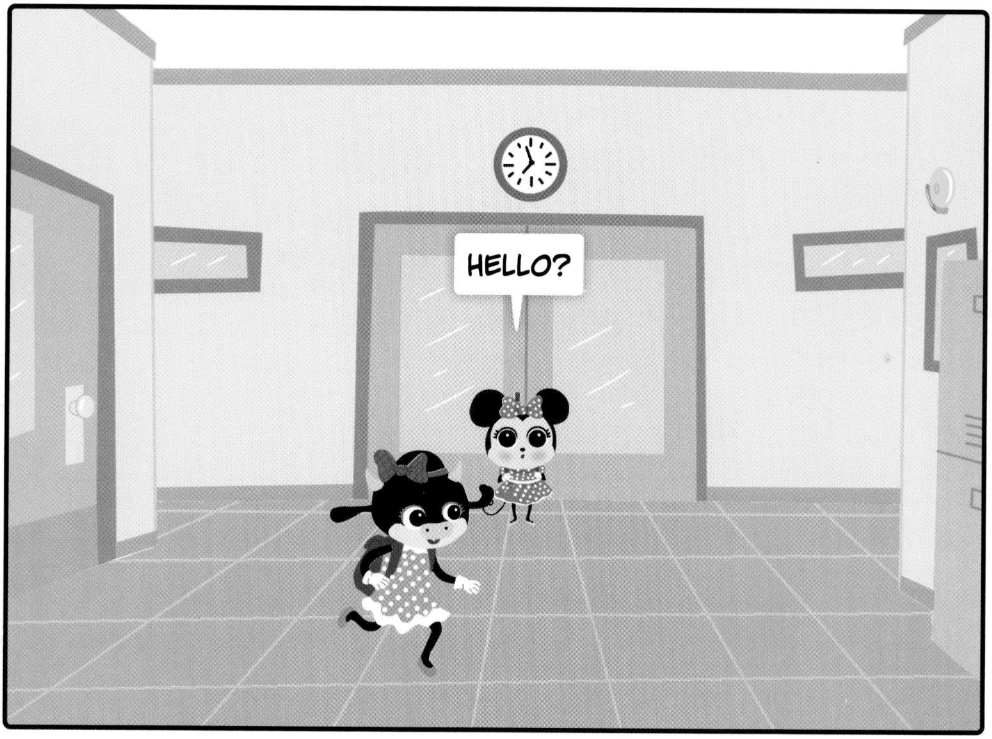
HELLO?

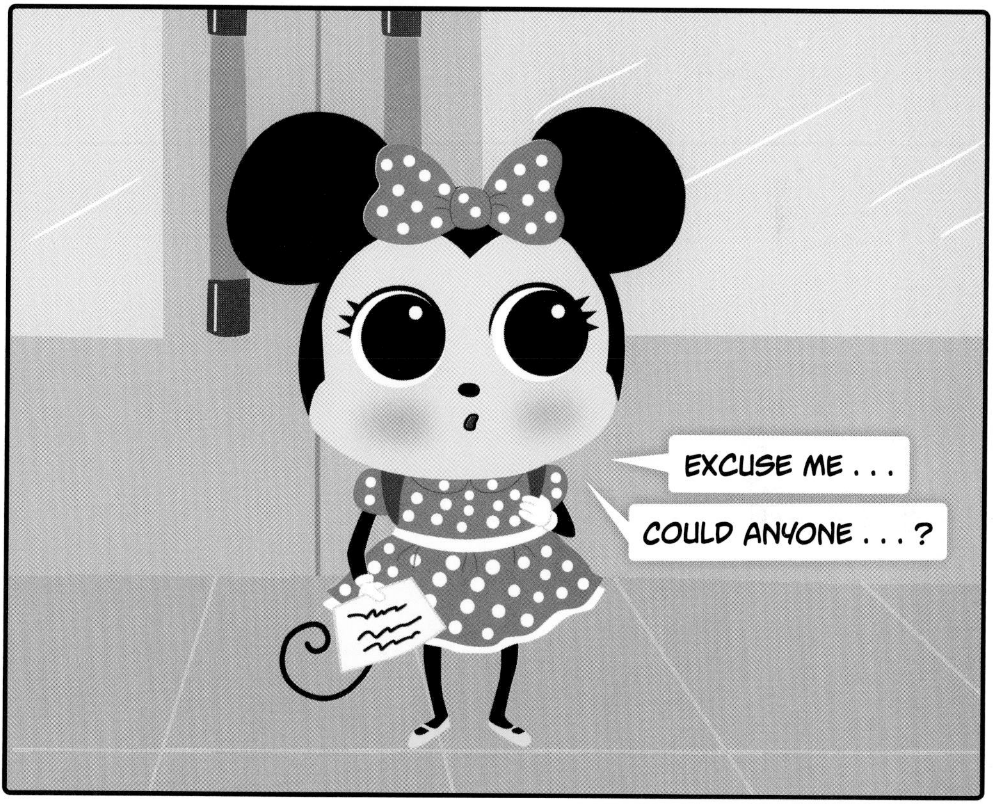
EXCUSE ME . . .
COULD ANYONE . . . ?

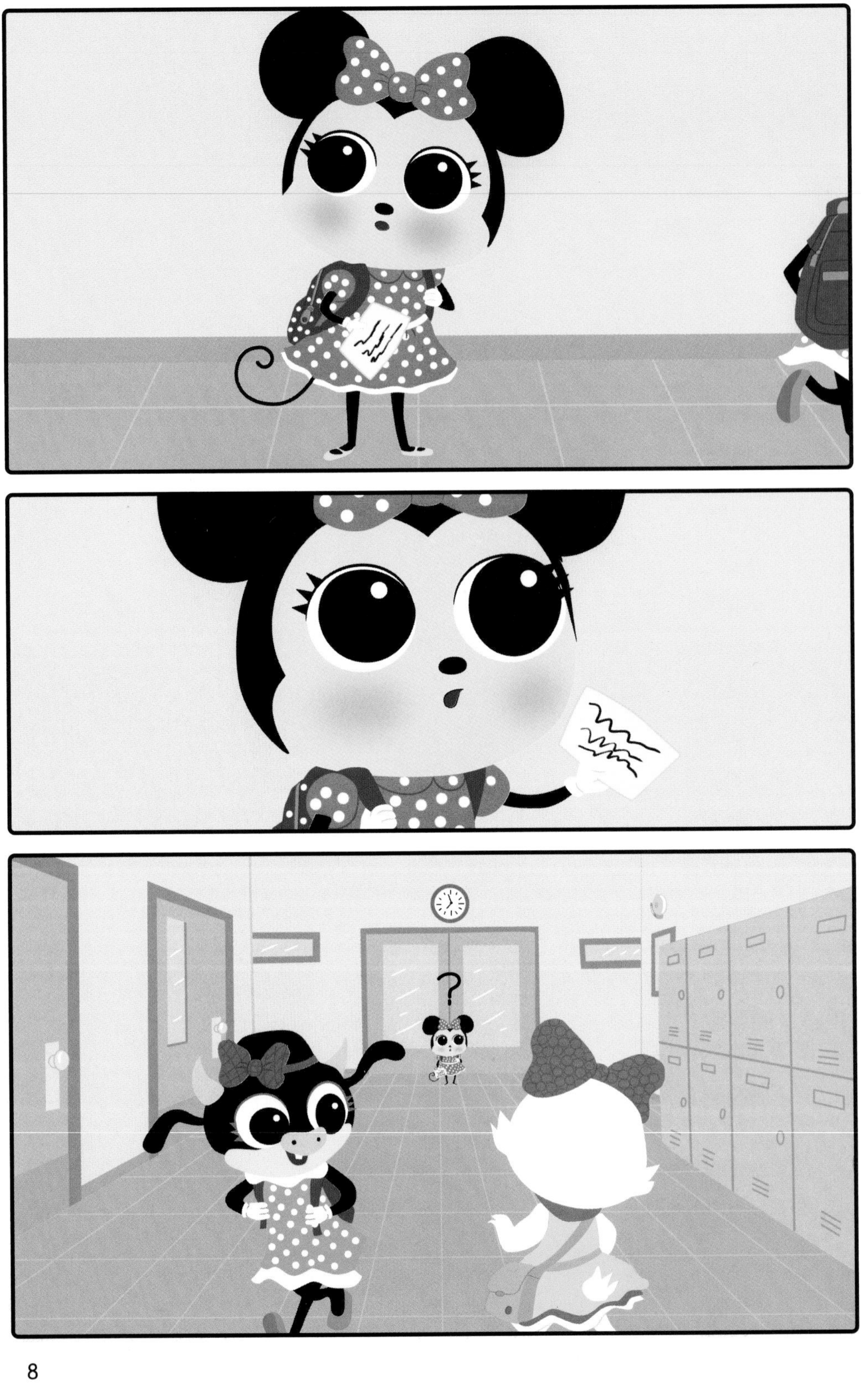
?

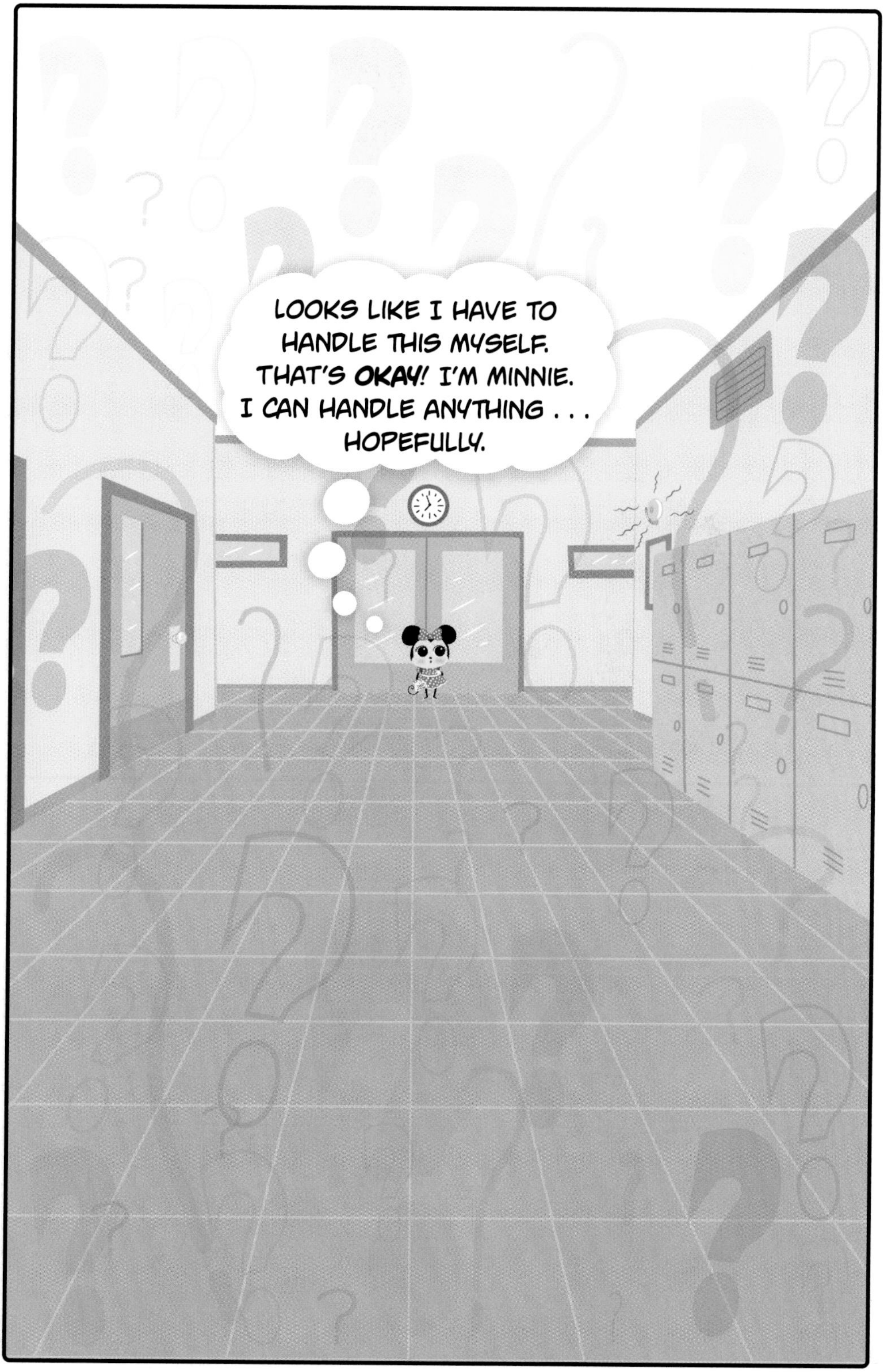
LOOKS LIKE I HAVE TO HANDLE THIS MYSELF. THAT'S **OKAY**! I'M MINNIE. I CAN HANDLE ANYTHING . . . HOPEFULLY.

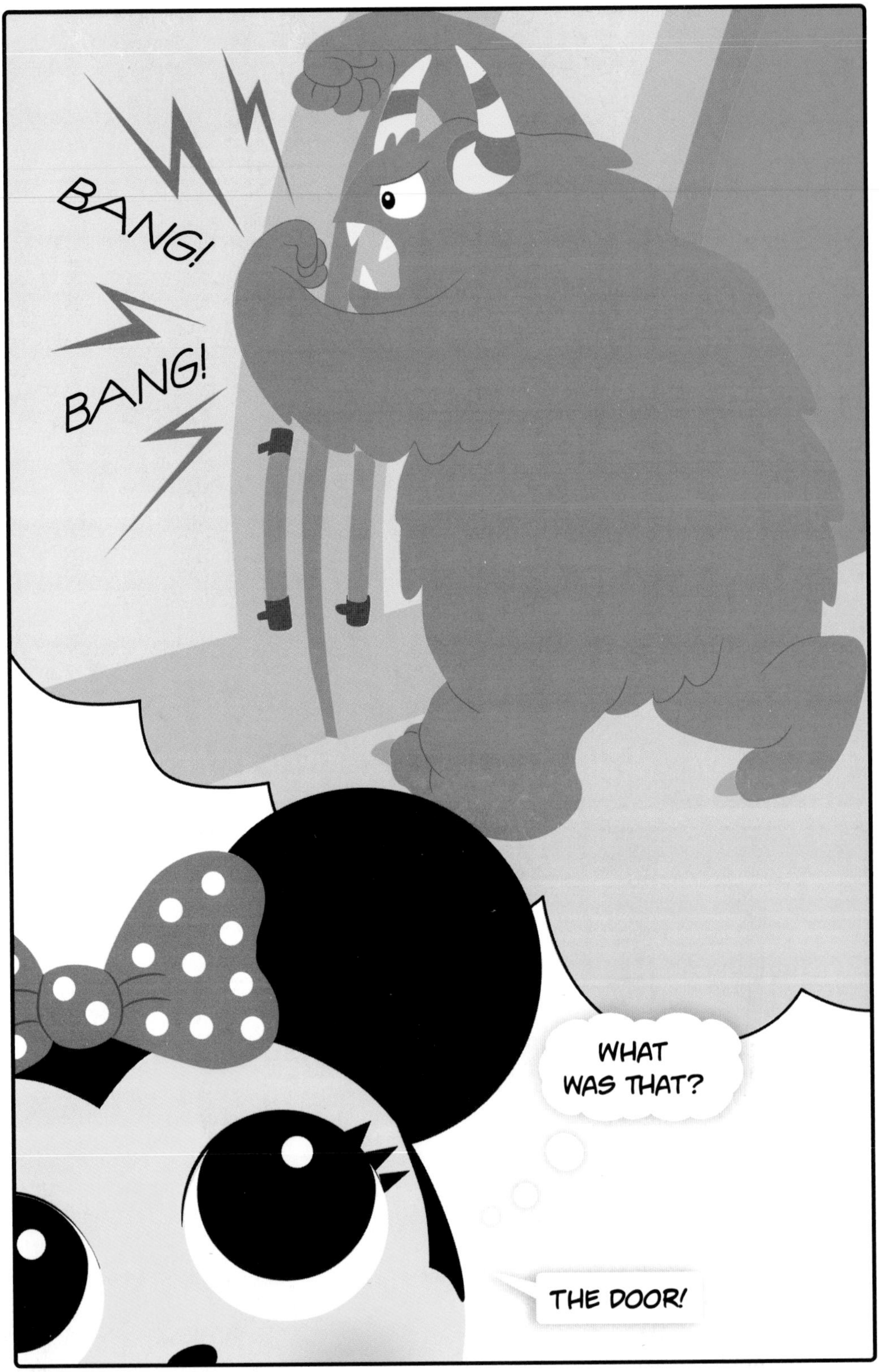
BANG!
BANG!
WHAT WAS THAT?
THE DOOR!

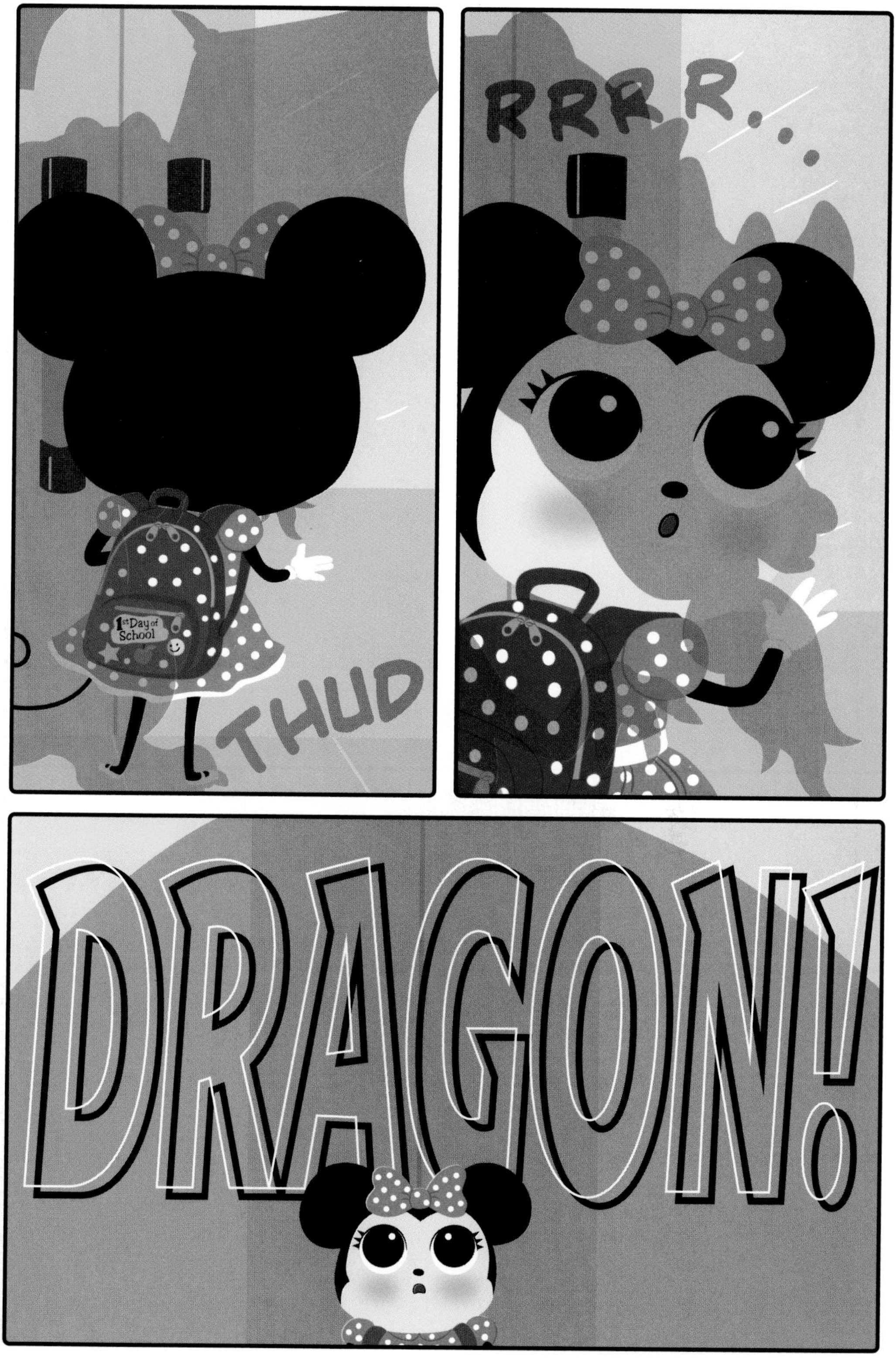
1st Day of School
THUD
RRRR...
DRAGON!

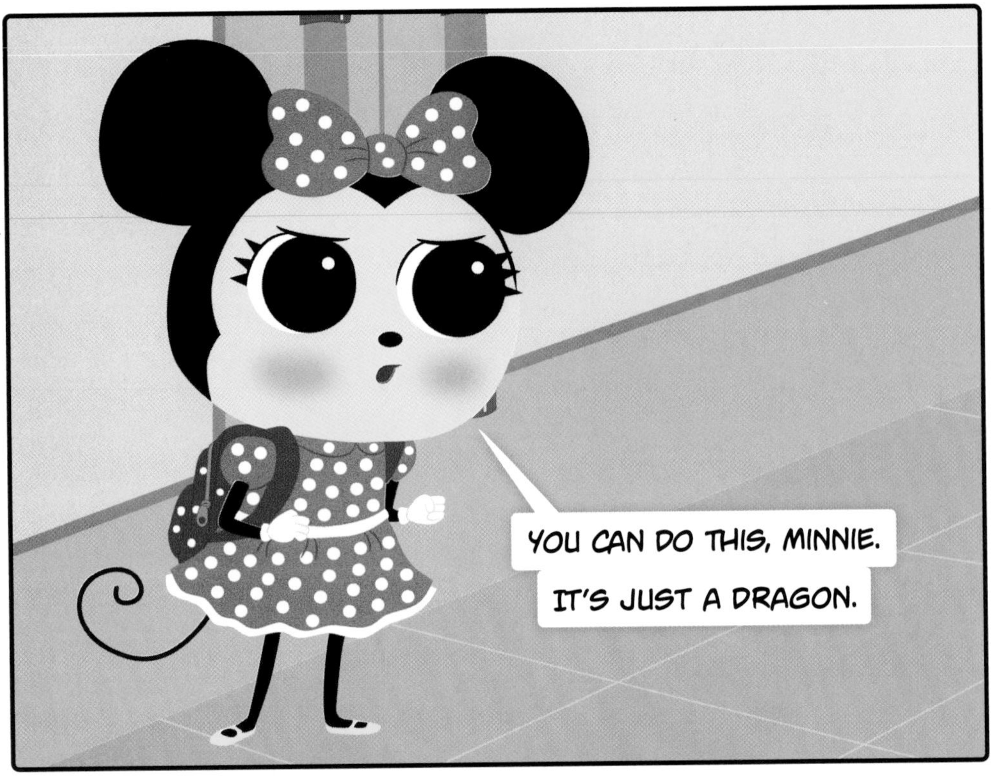
YOU CAN DO THIS, MINNIE.
IT'S JUST A DRAGON.

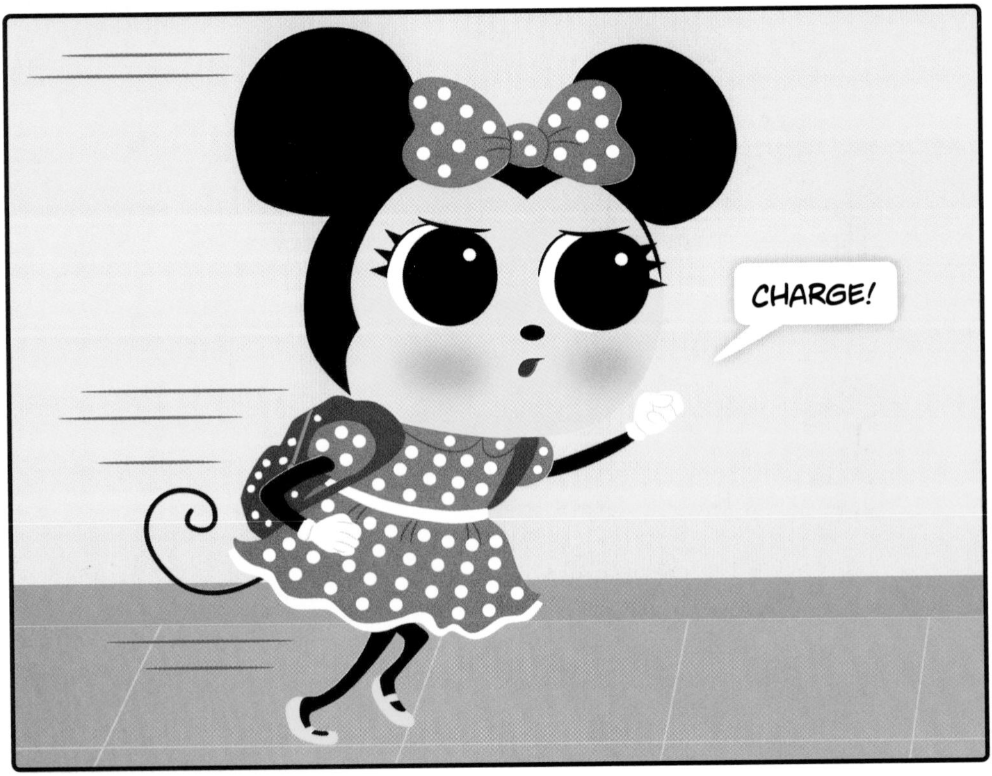
CHARGE!

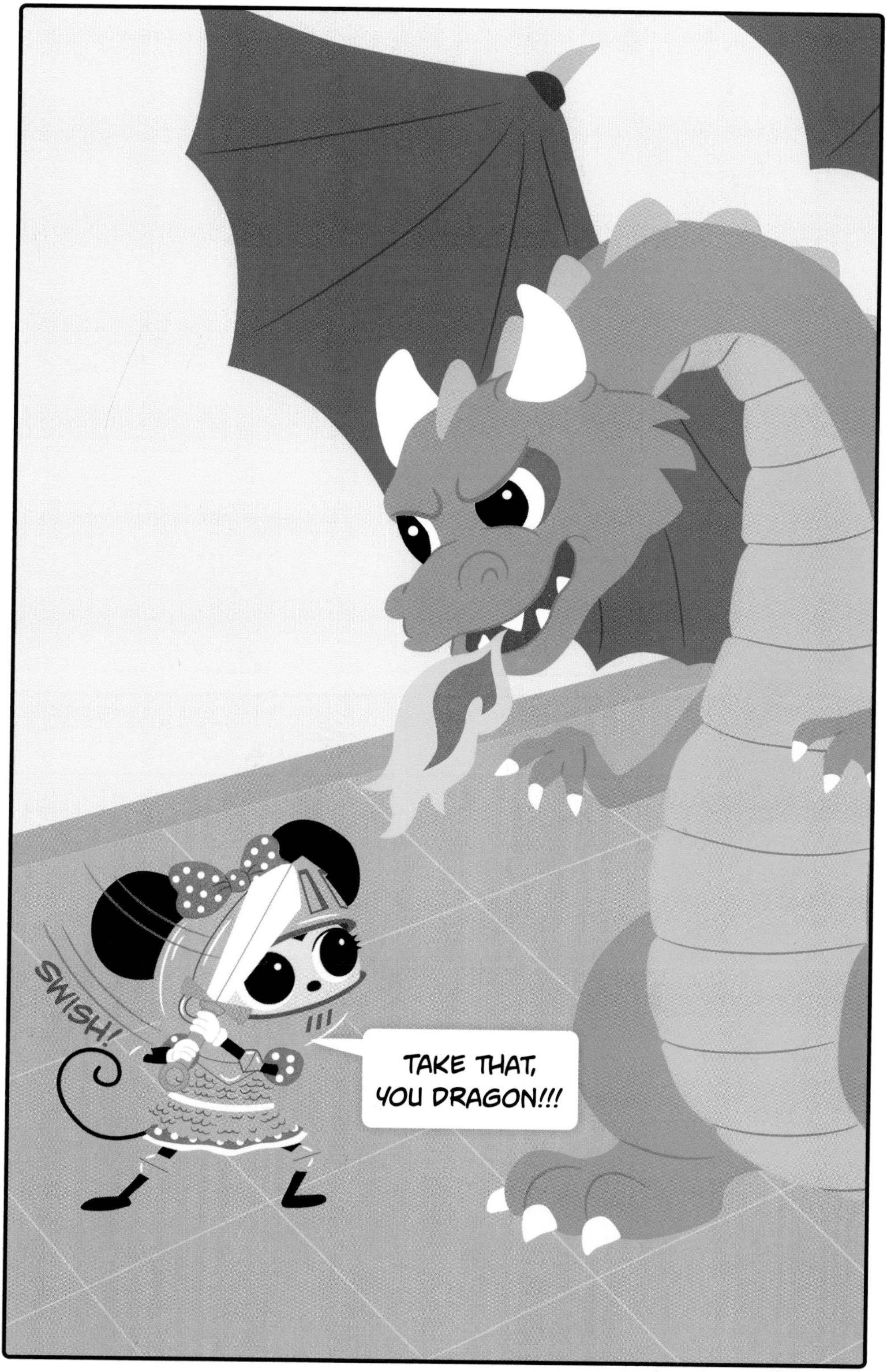
SWISH!
TAKE THAT, YOU DRAGON!!!

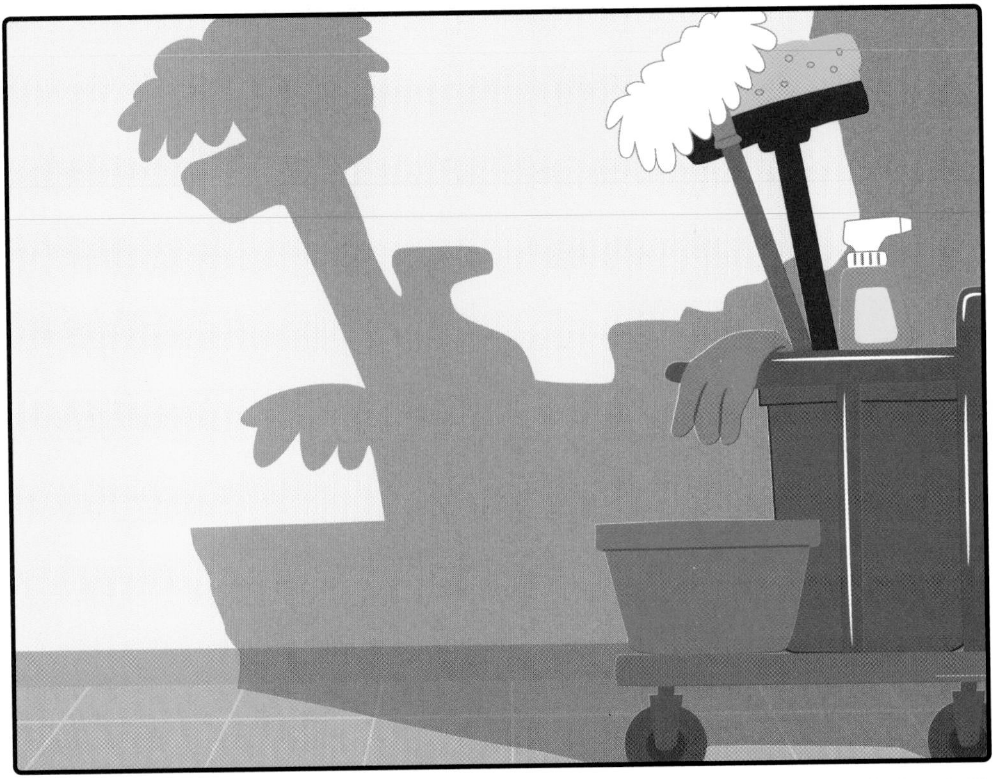

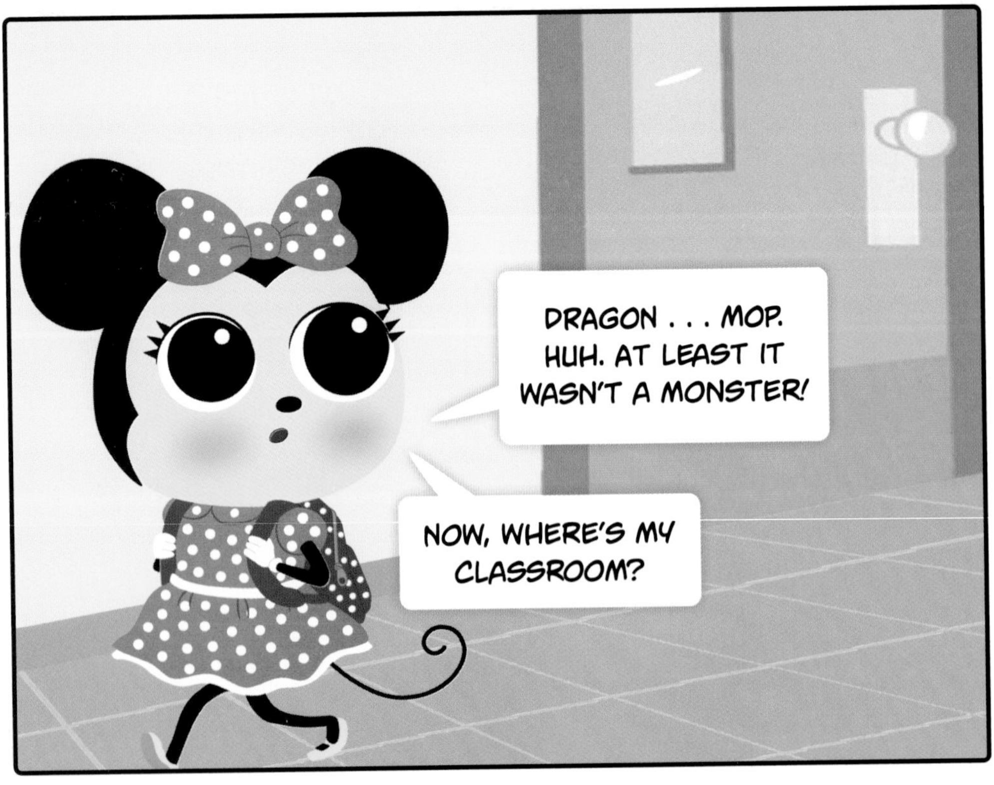
DRAGON . . . MOP. HUH. AT LEAST IT WASN'T A MONSTER!
NOW, WHERE'S MY CLASSROOM?

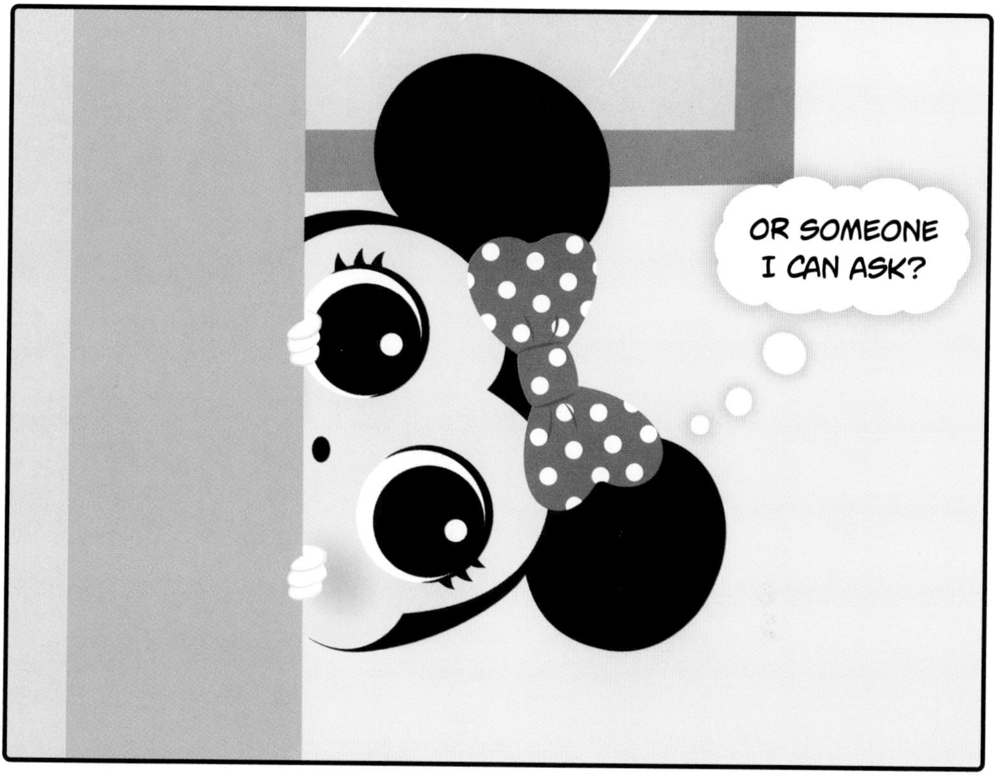
OR SOMEONE I CAN ASK?

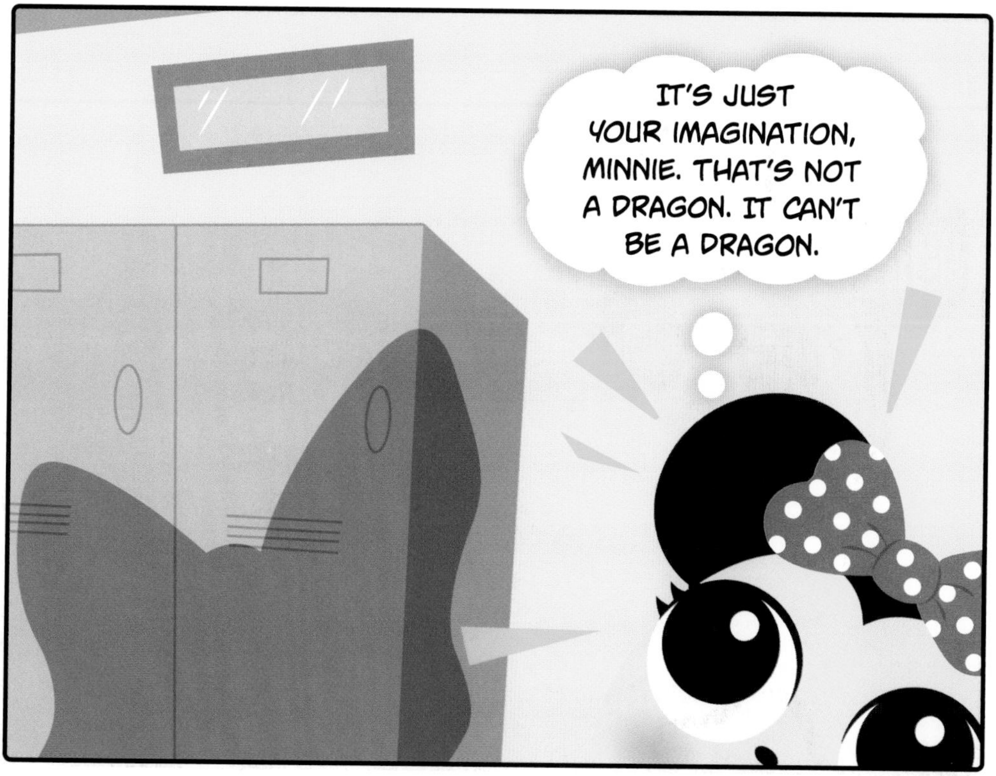
IT'S JUST YOUR IMAGINATION, MINNIE. THAT'S NOT A DRAGON. IT CAN'T BE A DRAGON.

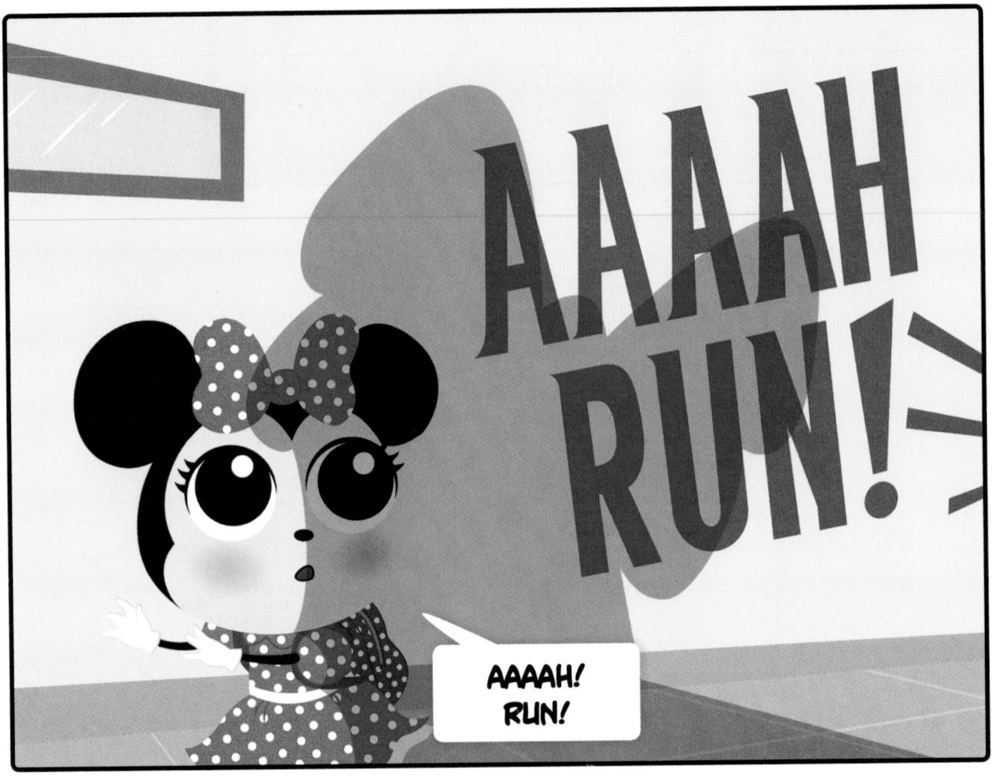
AAAAH
RUN!
AAAAH!
RUN!

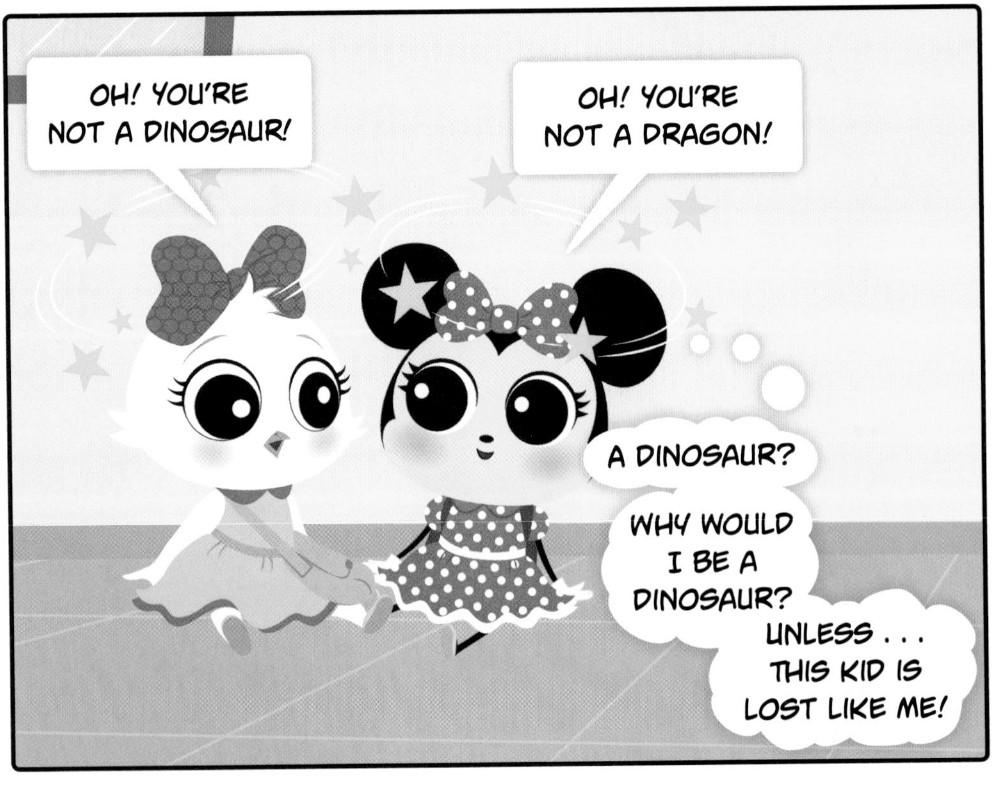
OH! YOU'RE
NOT A DINOSAUR!
OH! YOU'RE
NOT A DRAGON!
A DINOSAUR?
WHY WOULD
I BE A
DINOSAUR?
UNLESS . . .
THIS KID IS
LOST LIKE ME!

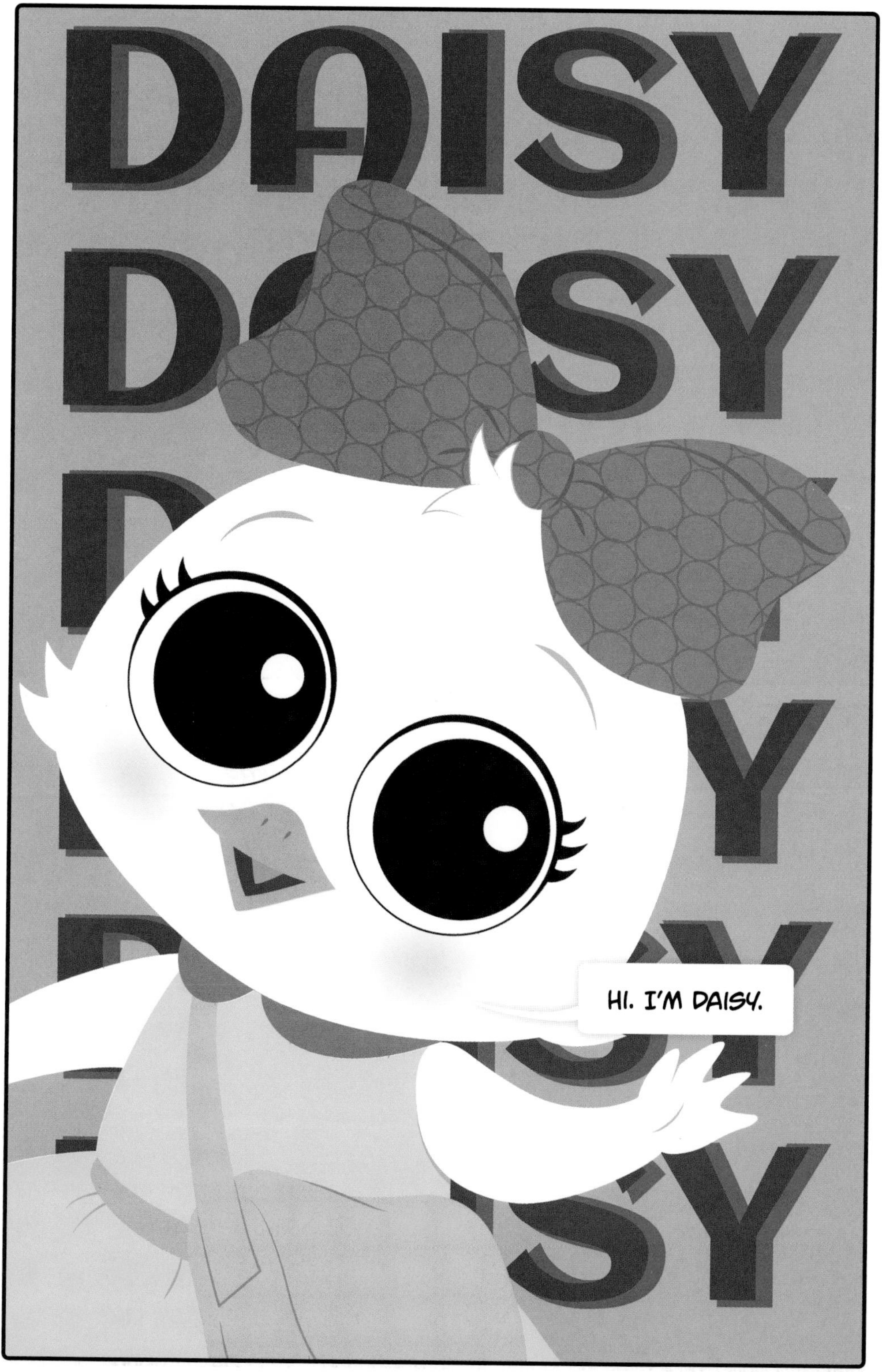
DAISY
DAISY
DAISY
DAISY
DAISY
DAISY
HI. I'M DAISY.

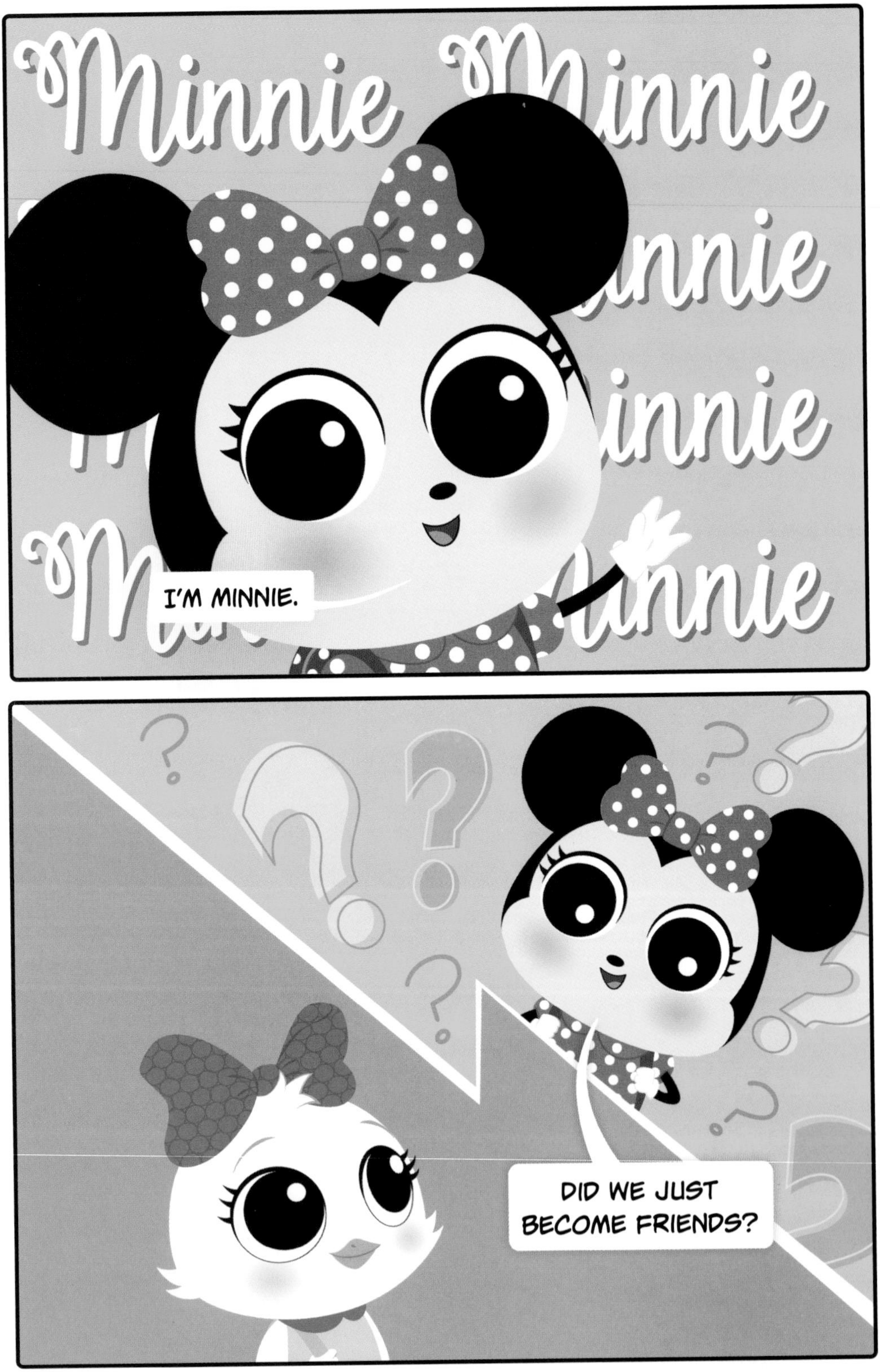
Minnie Minnie
Minnie
Minnie
Minnie Minnie
I'M MINNIE.
DID WE JUST BECOME FRIENDS?

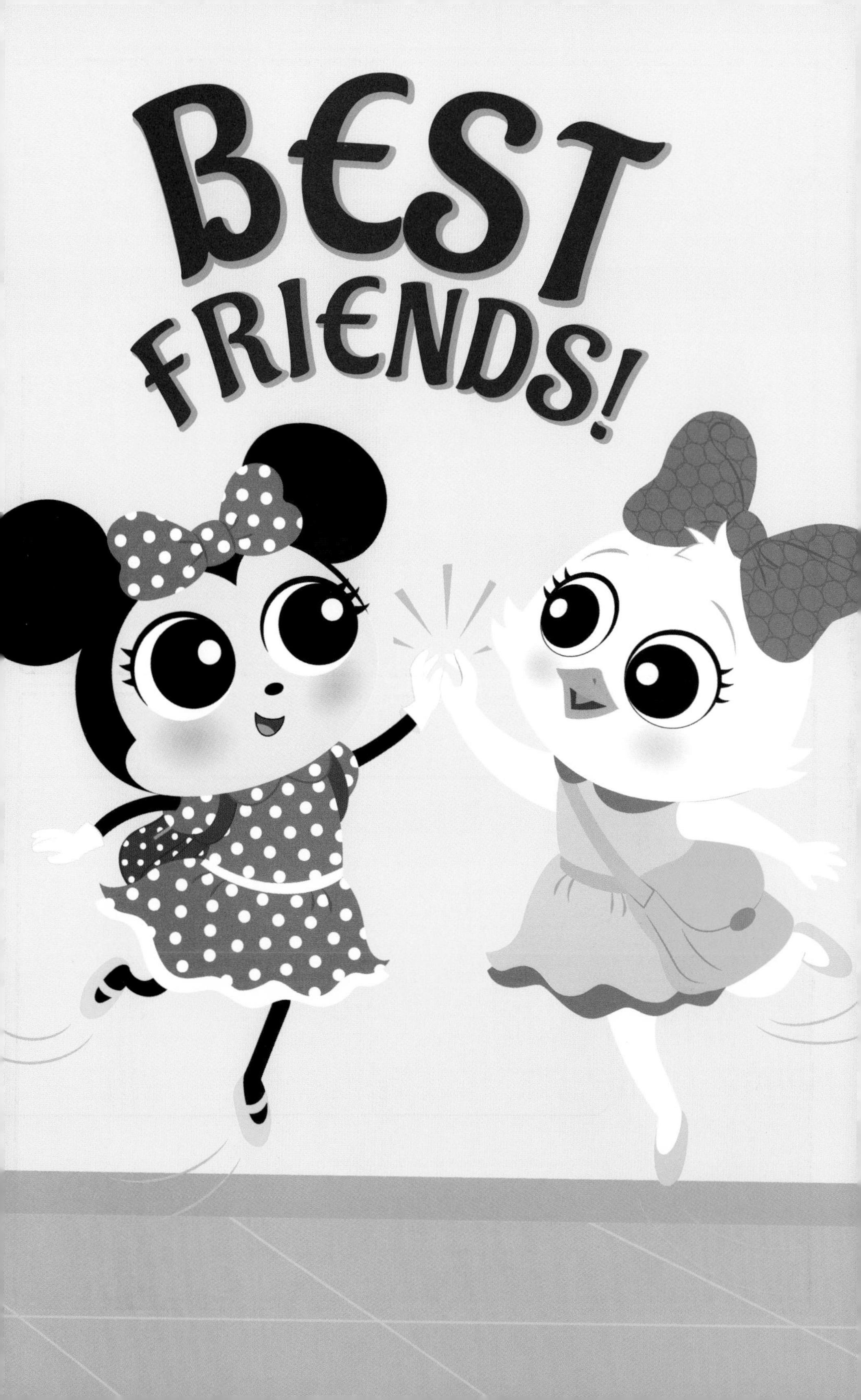
BEST
FRIENDS!

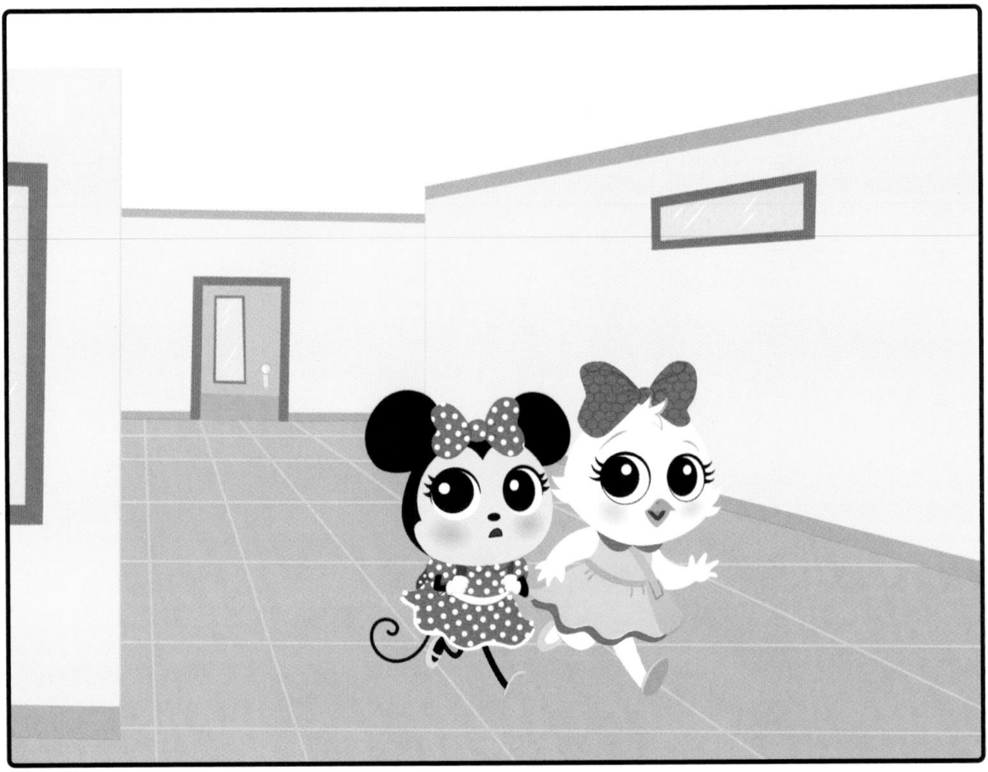

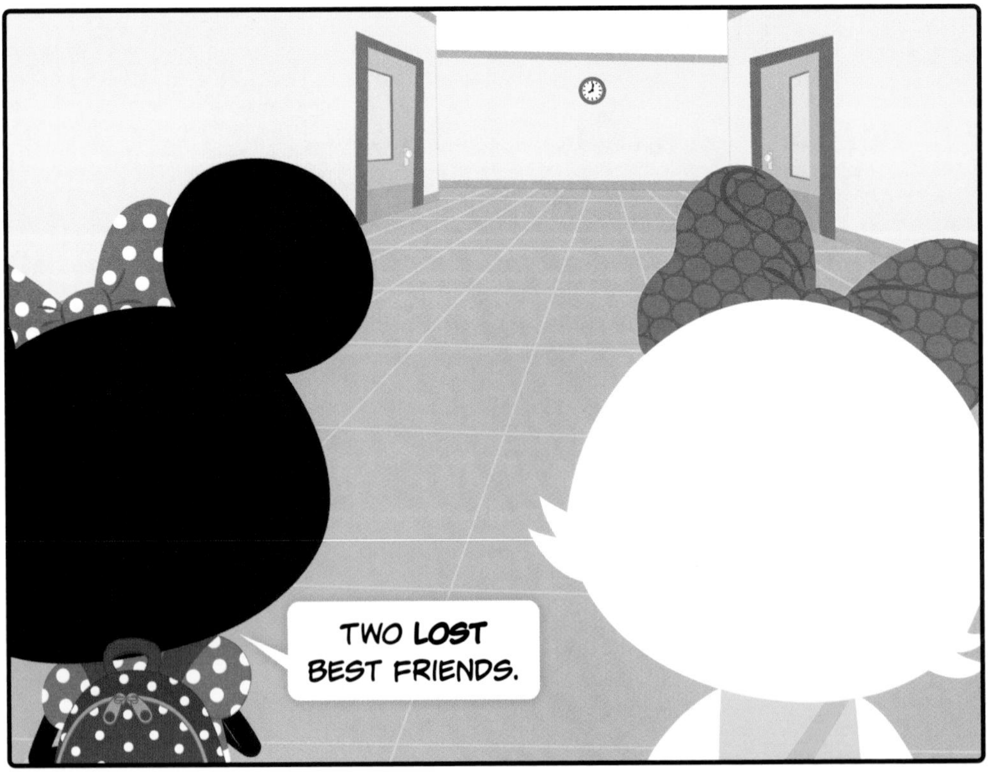
TWO LOST
BEST FRIENDS.

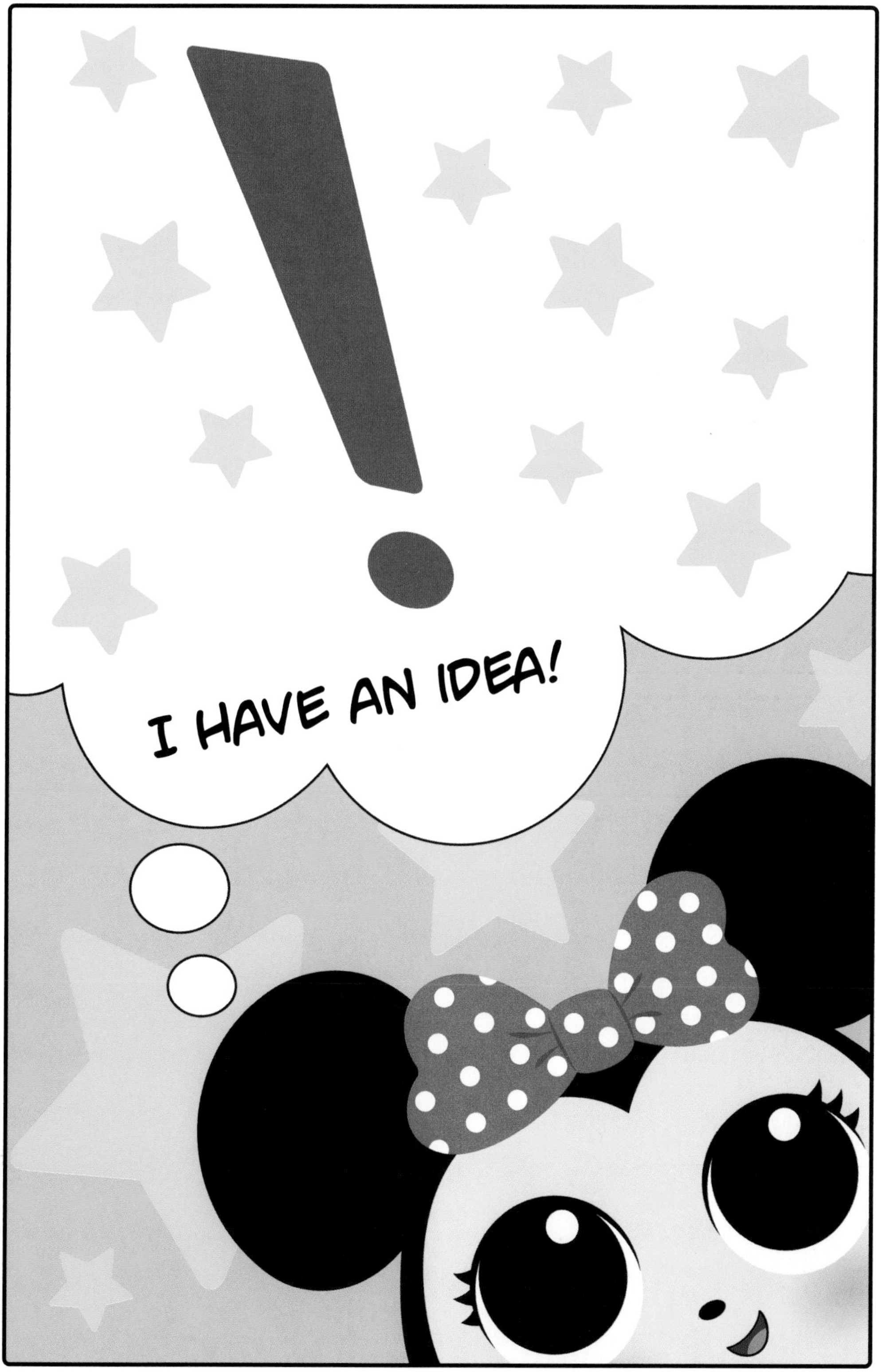
!
I HAVE AN IDEA!

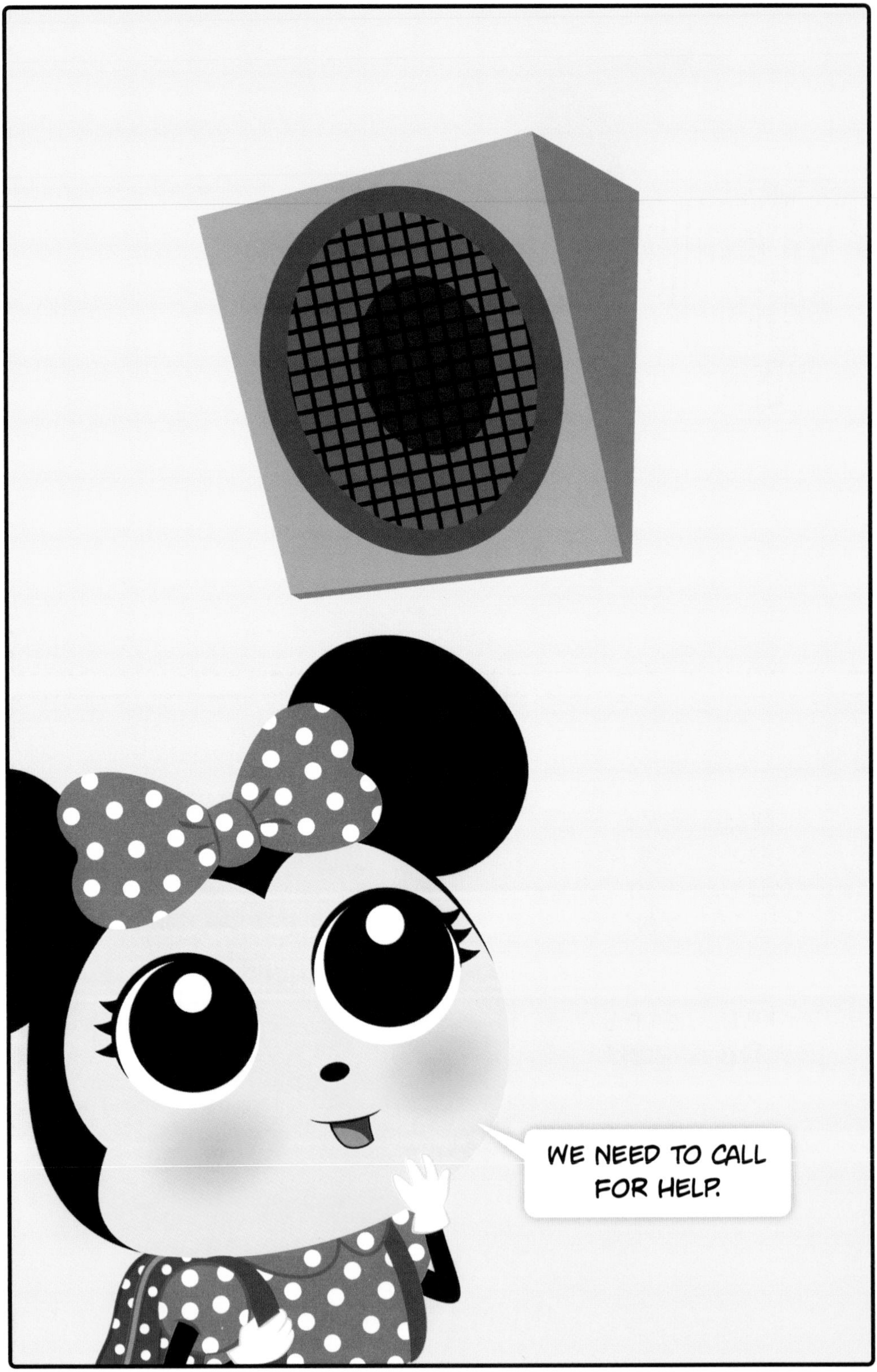
WE NEED TO CALL FOR HELP.

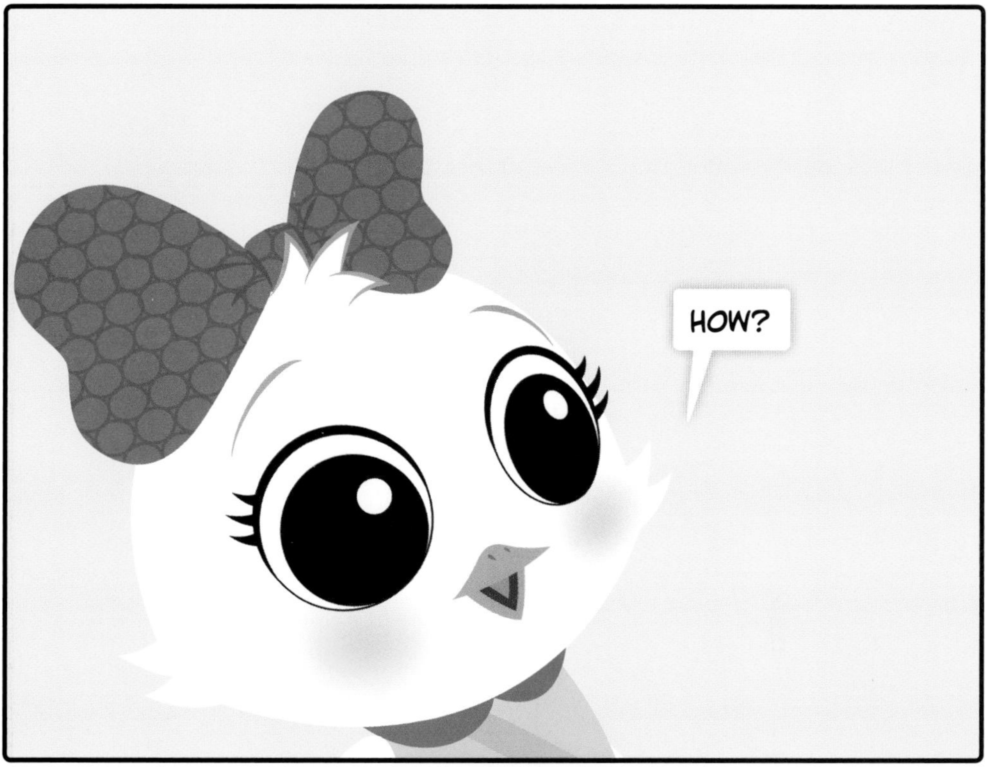
HOW?

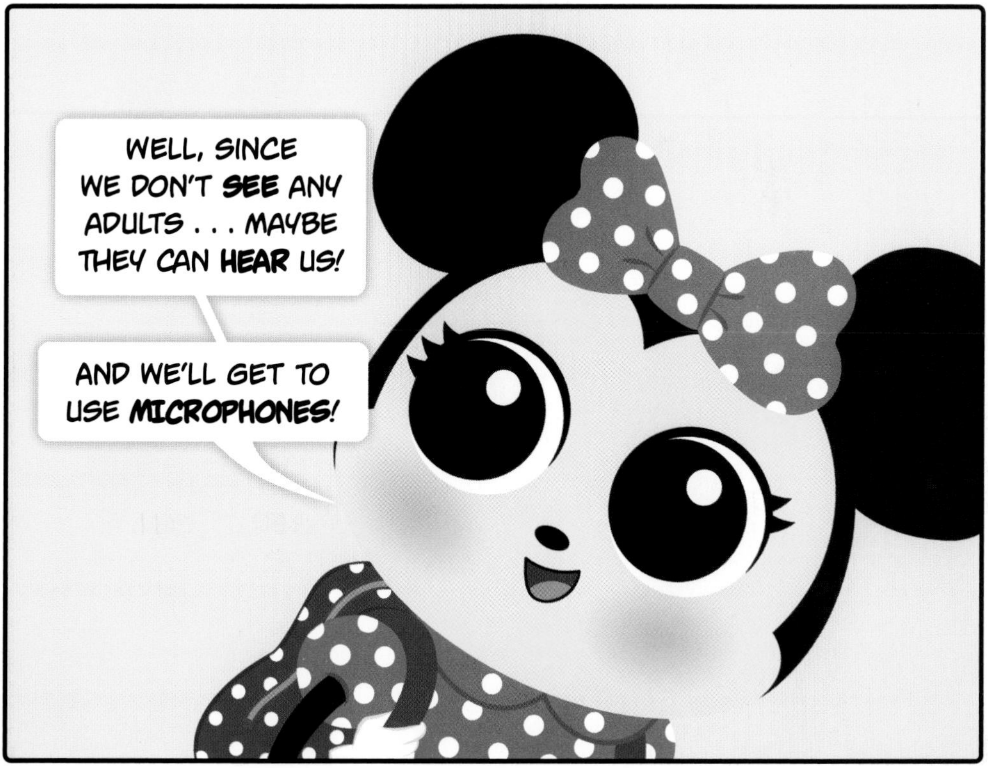
WELL, SINCE WE DON'T SEE ANY ADULTS . . . MAYBE THEY CAN HEAR US!
AND WE'LL GET TO USE MICROPHONES!

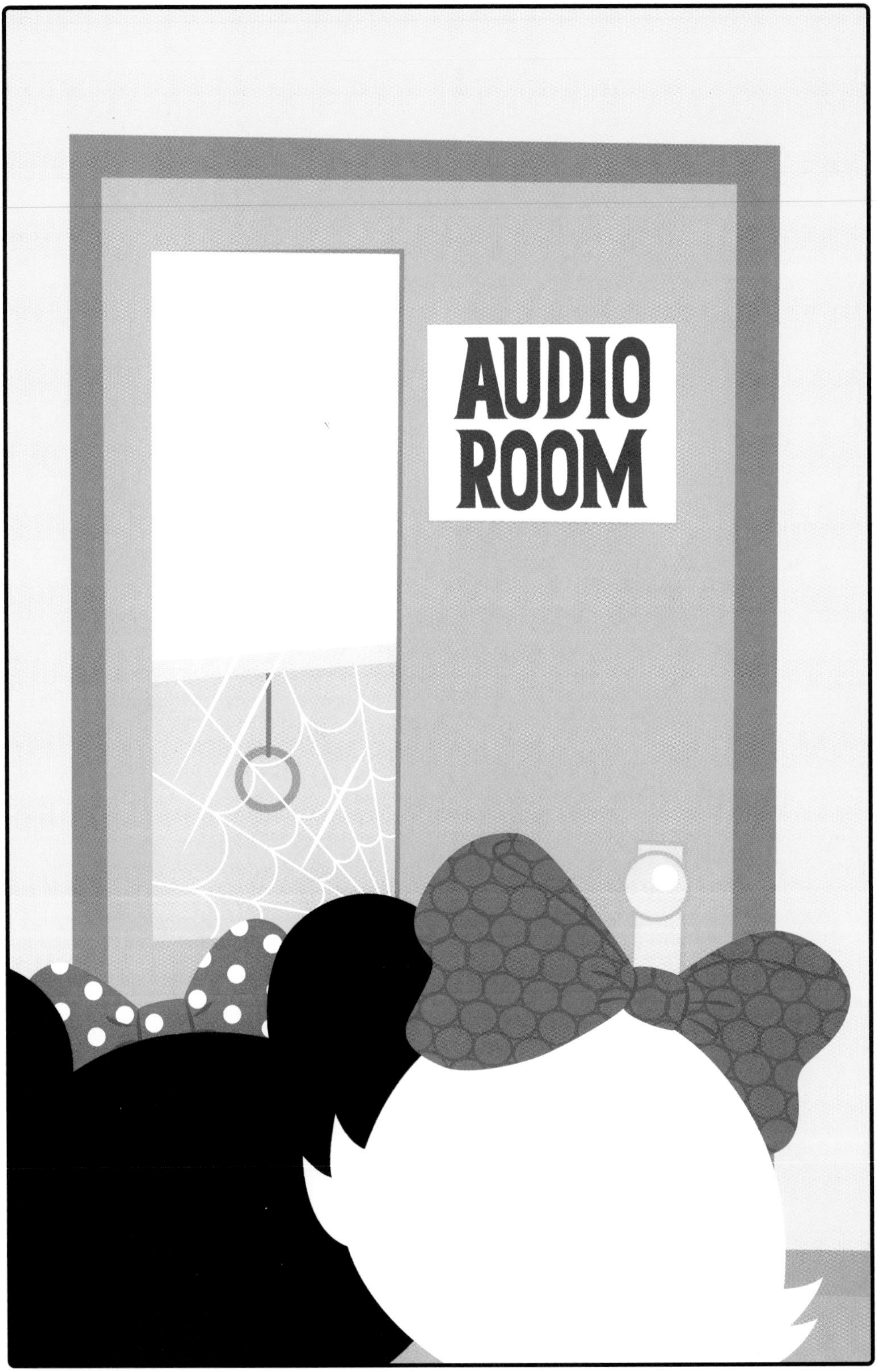
AUDIO
ROOM

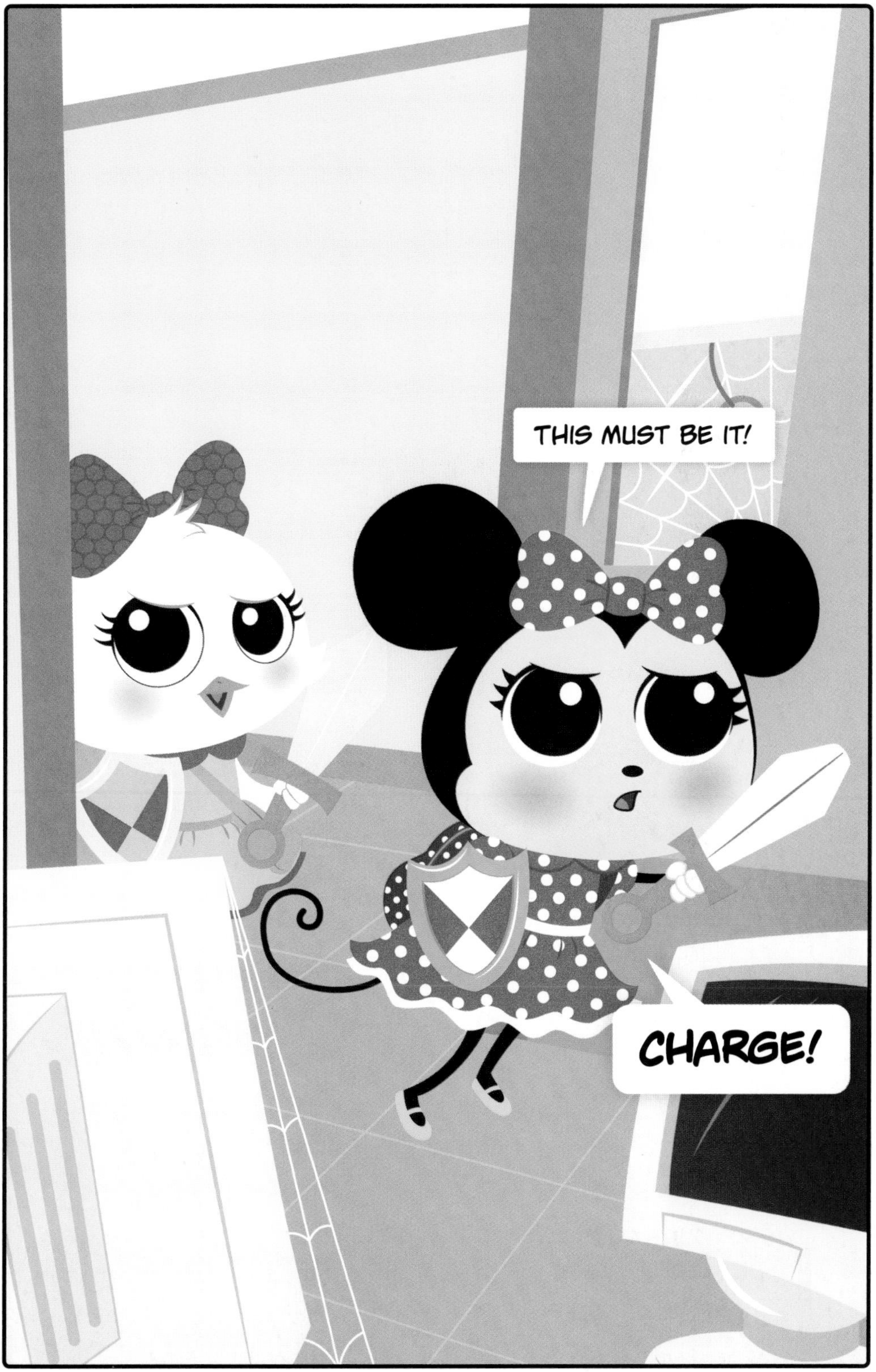
THIS MUST BE IT!
CHARGE!

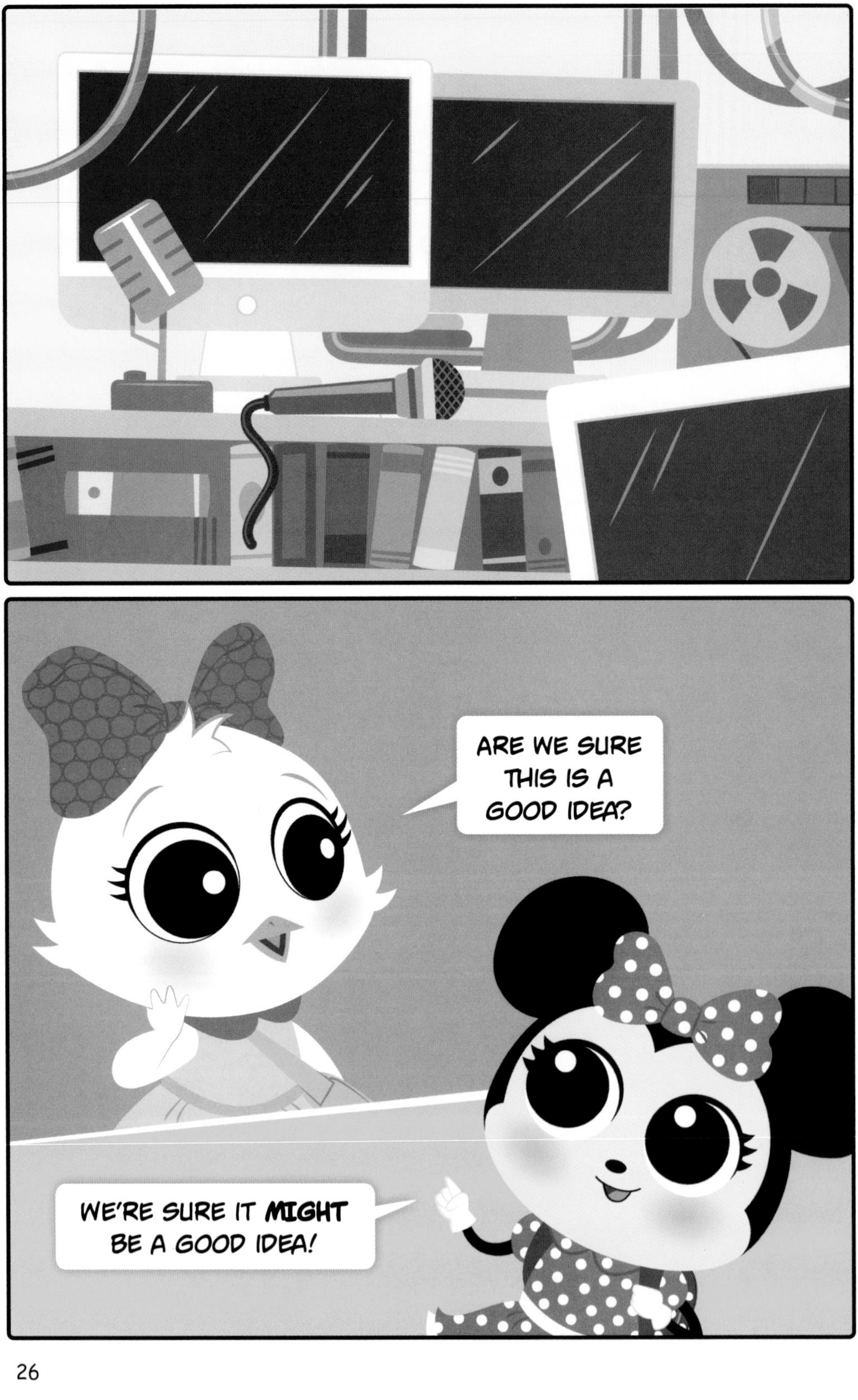
ARE WE SURE THIS IS A GOOD IDEA?
WE'RE SURE IT **MIGHT** BE A GOOD IDEA!

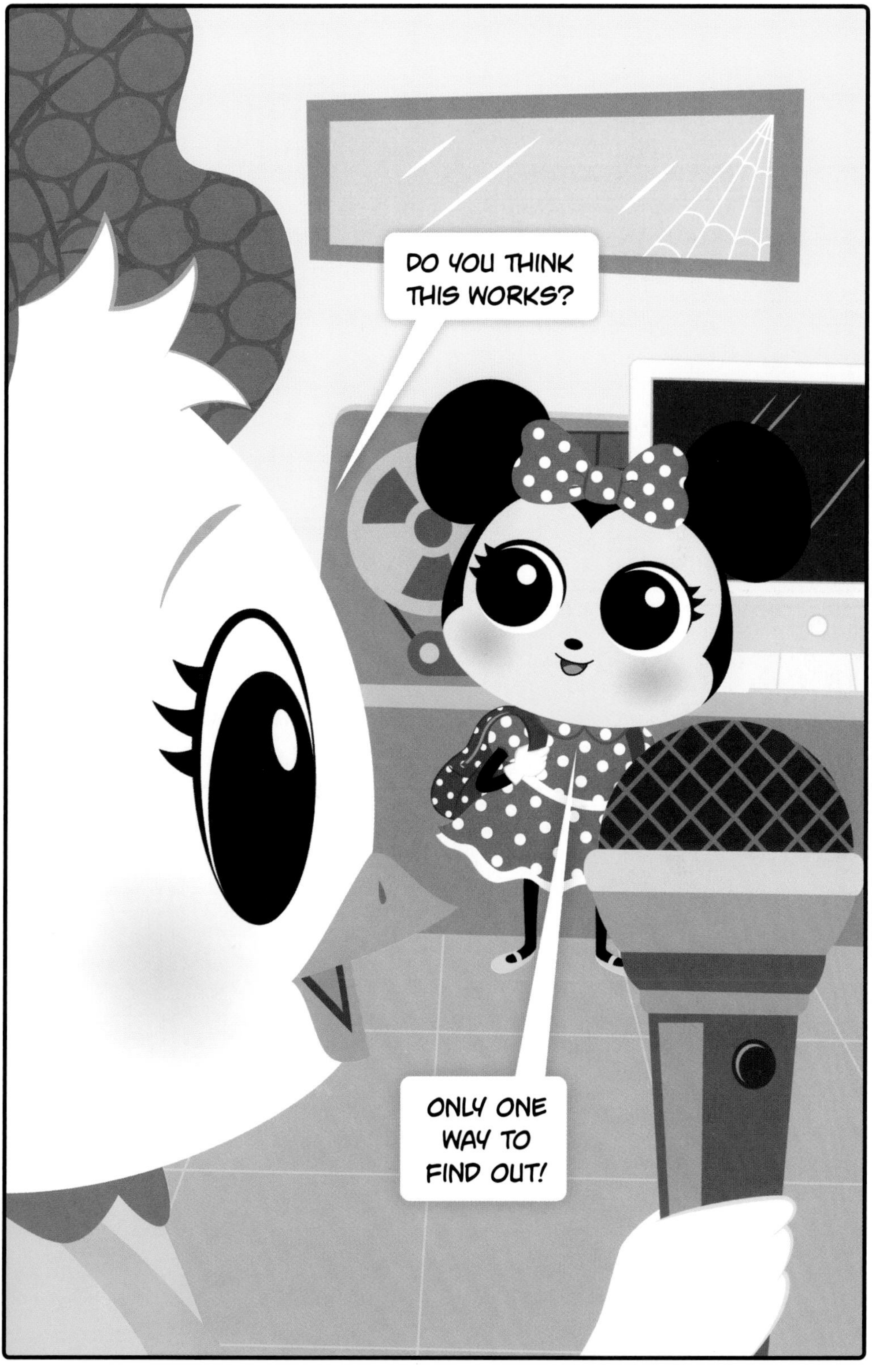
DO YOU THINK THIS WORKS?
ONLY ONE WAY TO FIND OUT!

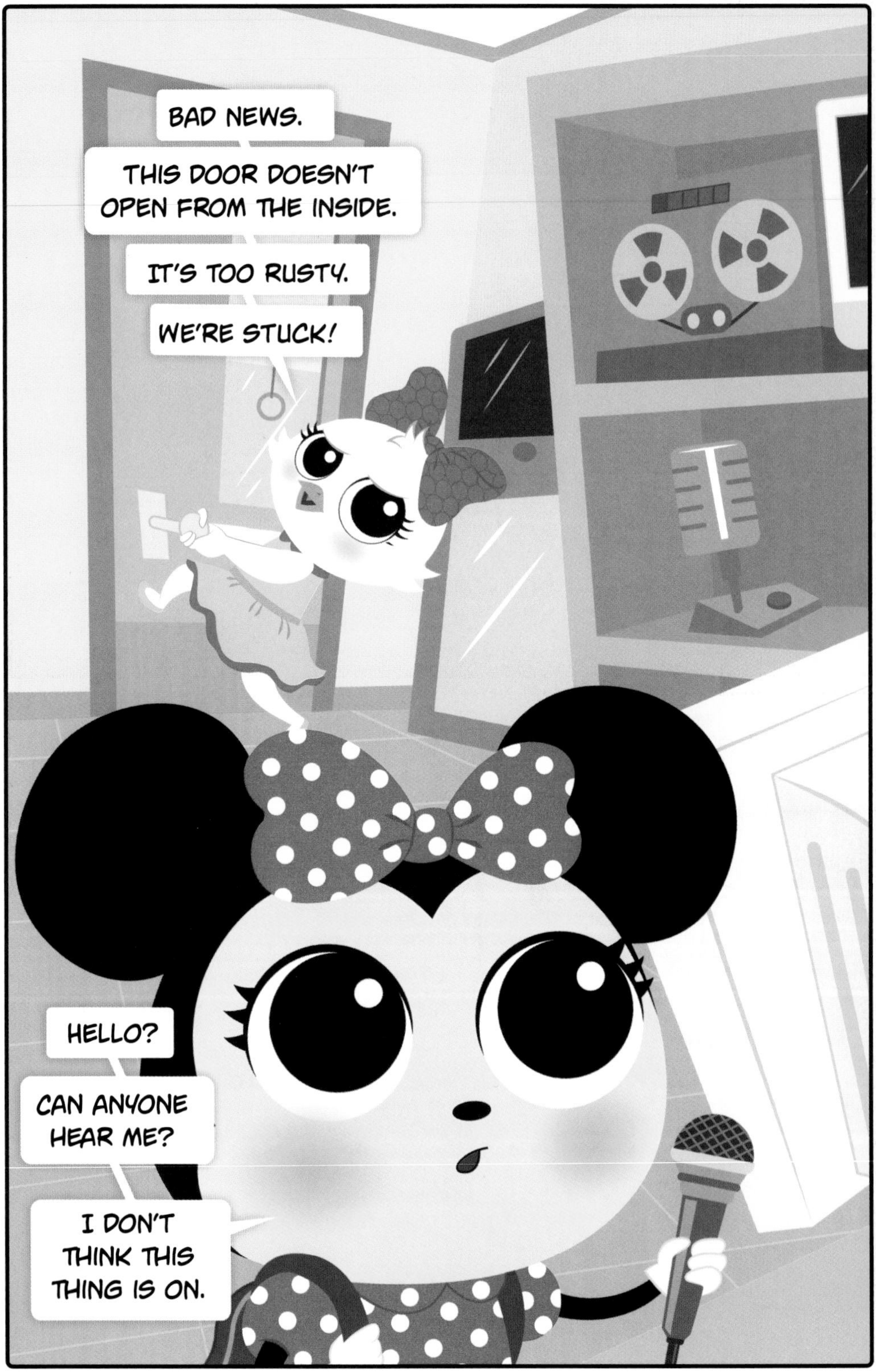
BAD NEWS.
THIS DOOR DOESN'T OPEN FROM THE INSIDE.
IT'S TOO RUSTY.
WE'RE STUCK!
HELLO?
CAN ANYONE HEAR ME?
I DON'T THINK THIS THING IS ON.

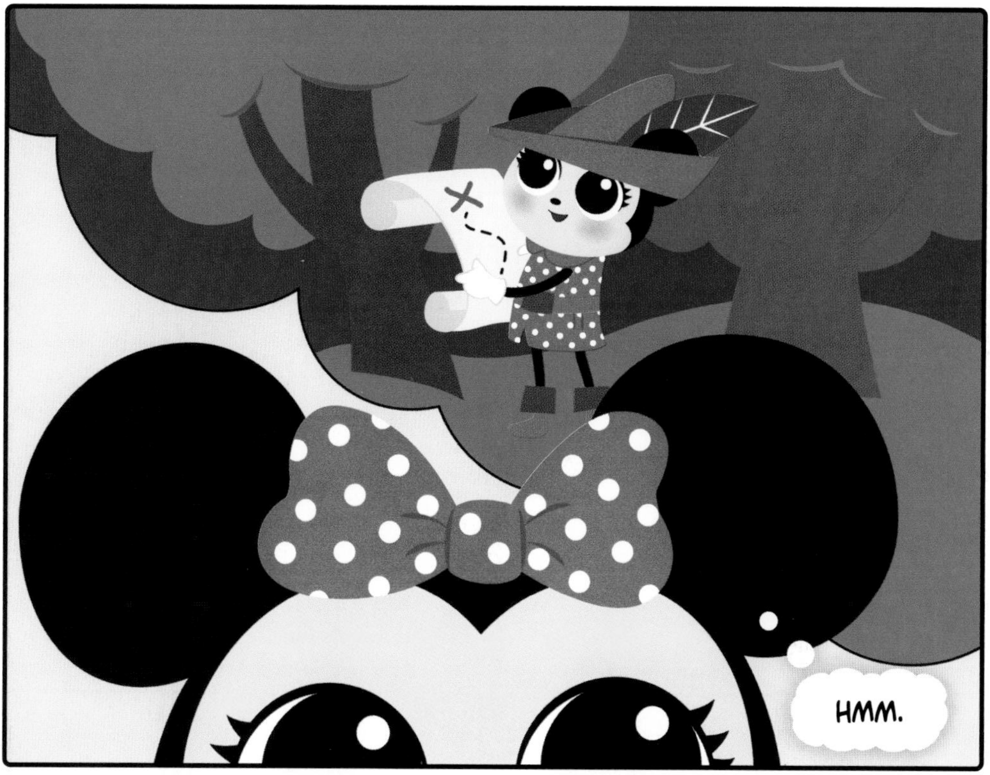
HMM.

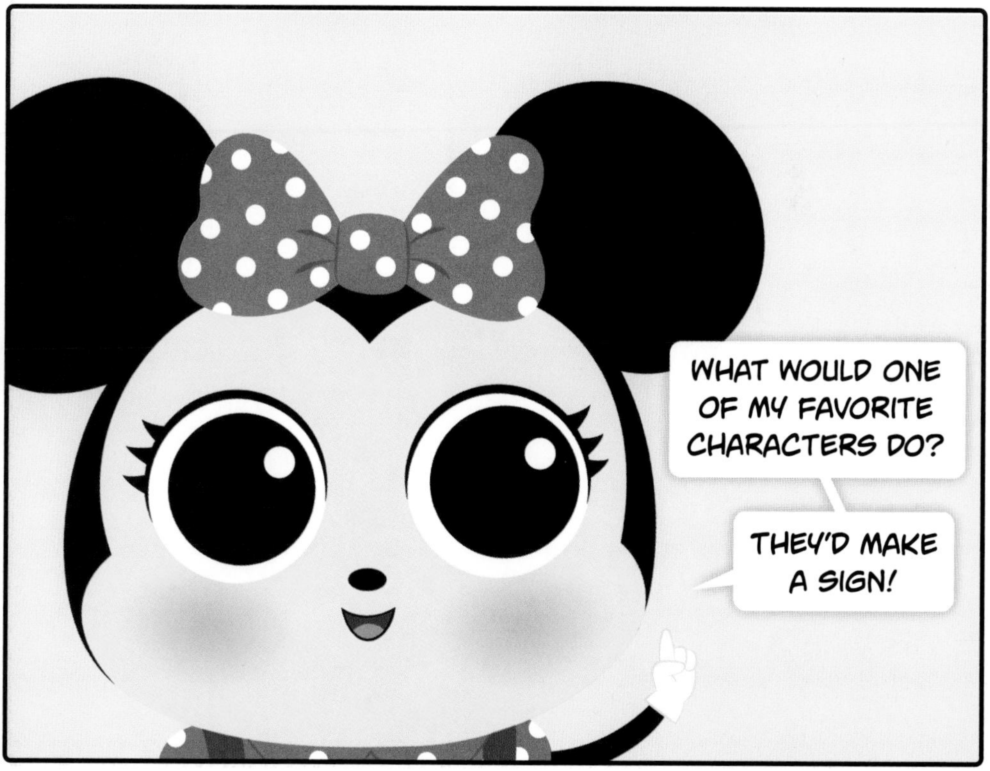
WHAT WOULD ONE OF MY FAVORITE CHARACTERS DO?
THEY'D MAKE A SIGN!

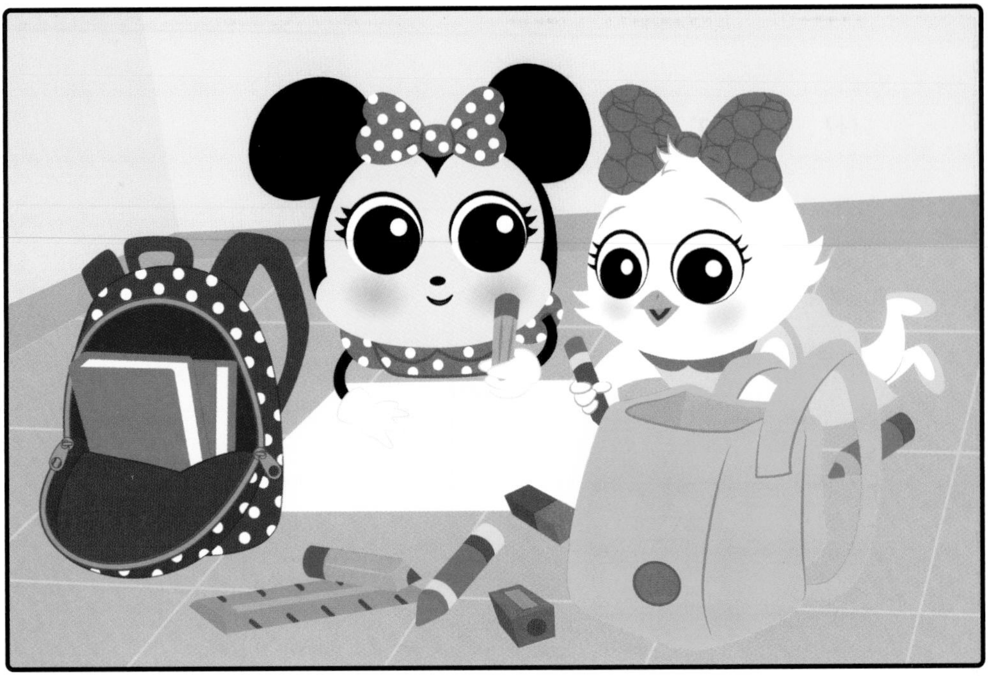

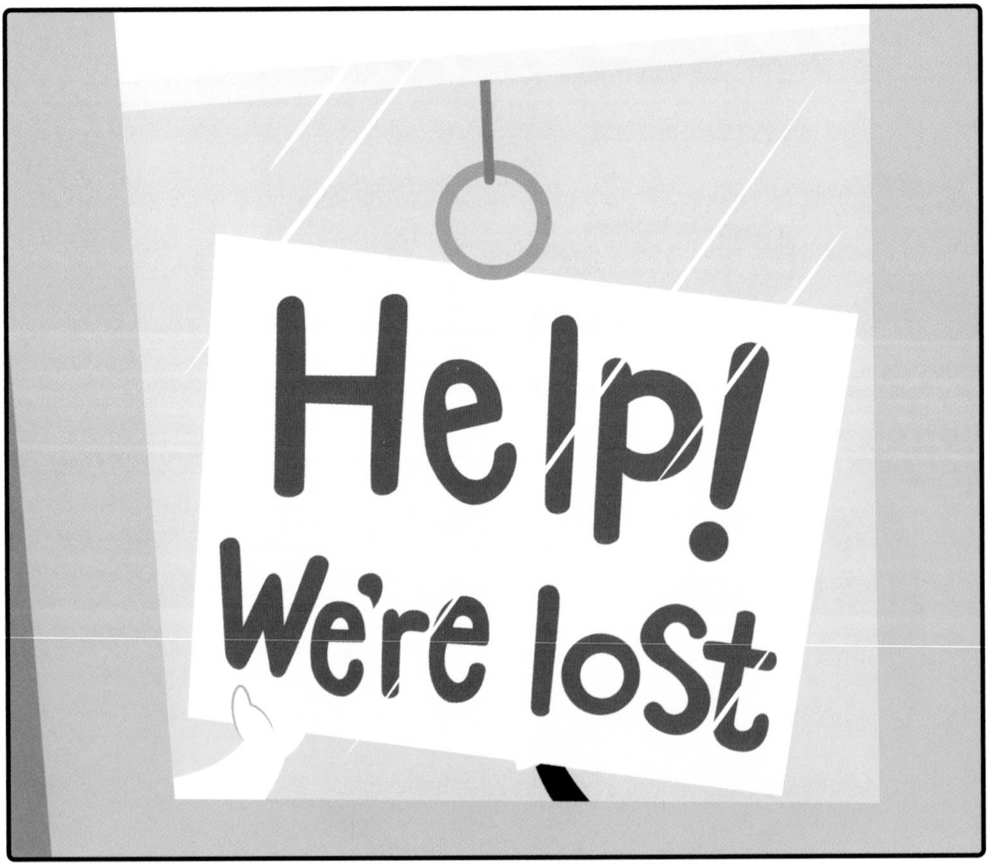
Help!
We're lost

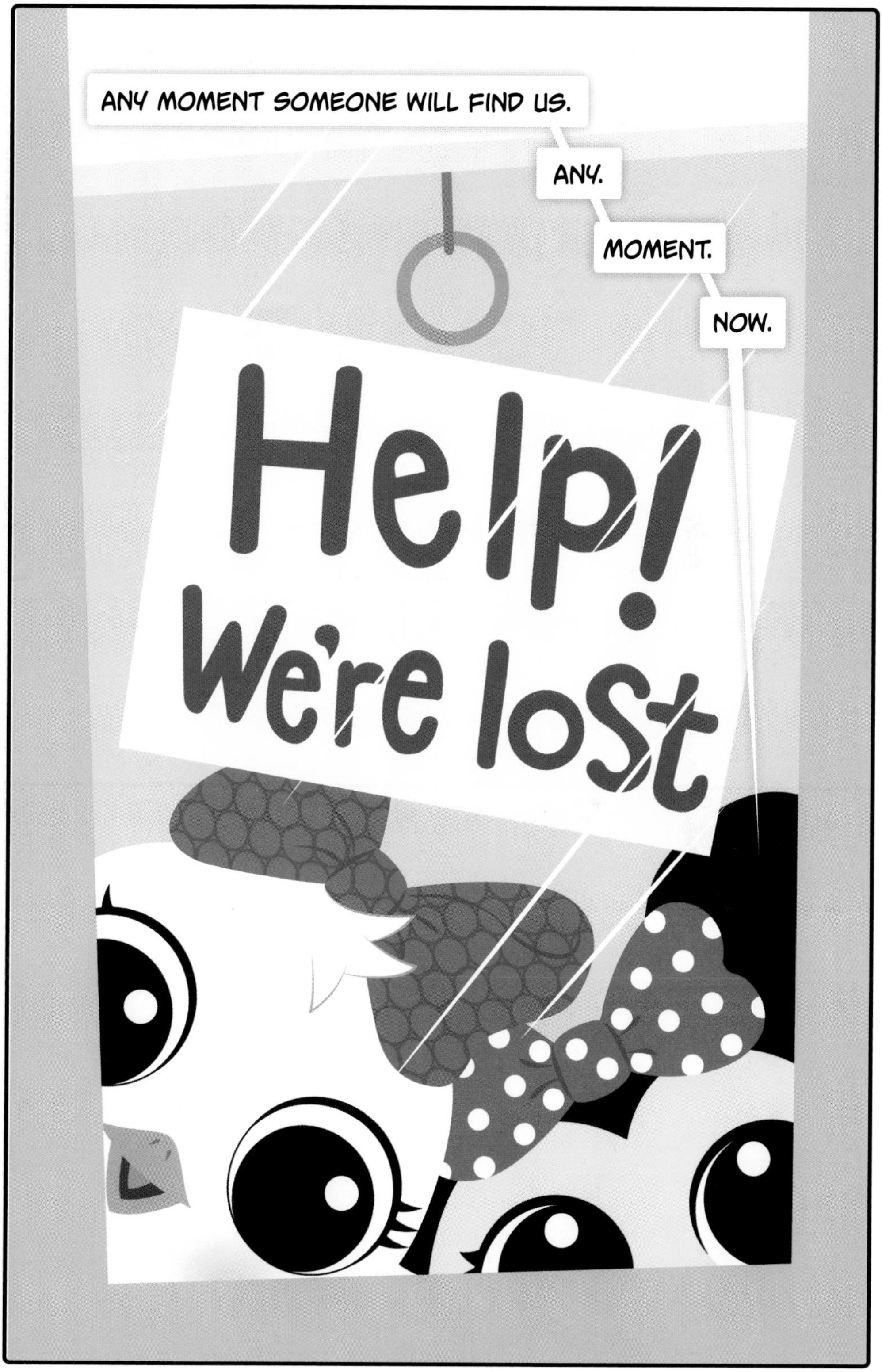
ANY MOMENT SOMEONE WILL FIND US.
ANY.
MOMENT.
NOW.
Help! We're lost

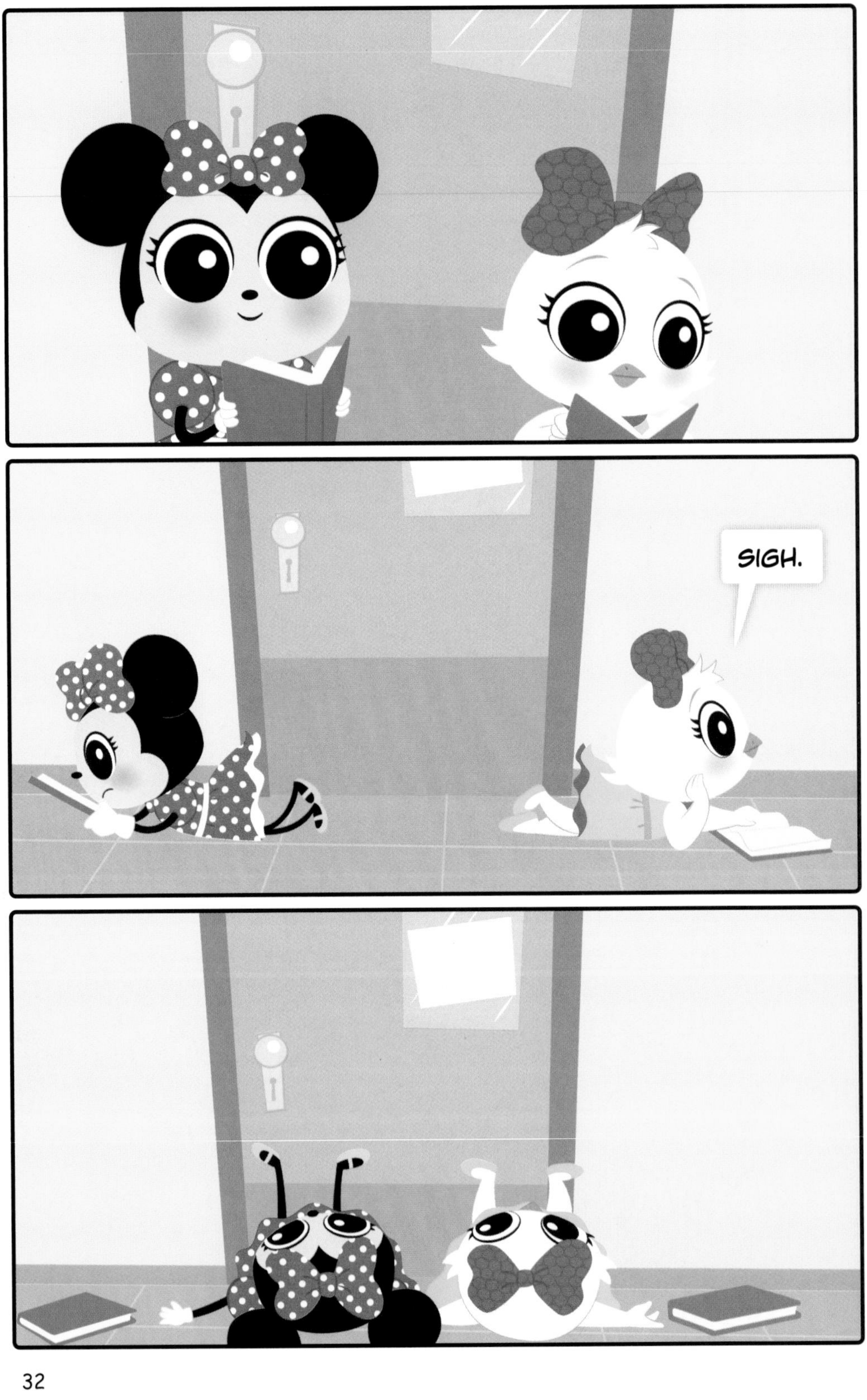
SIGH.

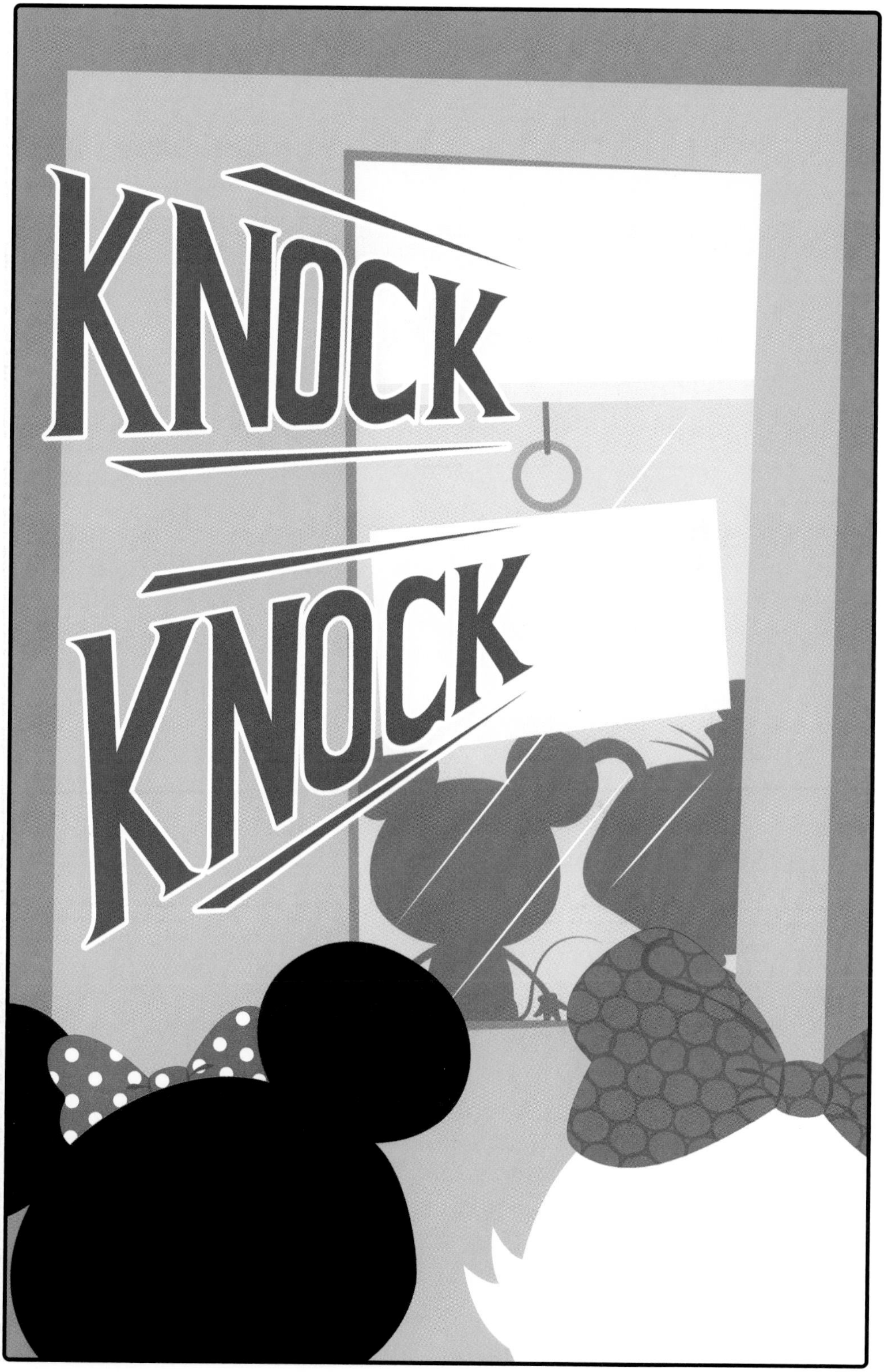
KNOCK
KNOCK

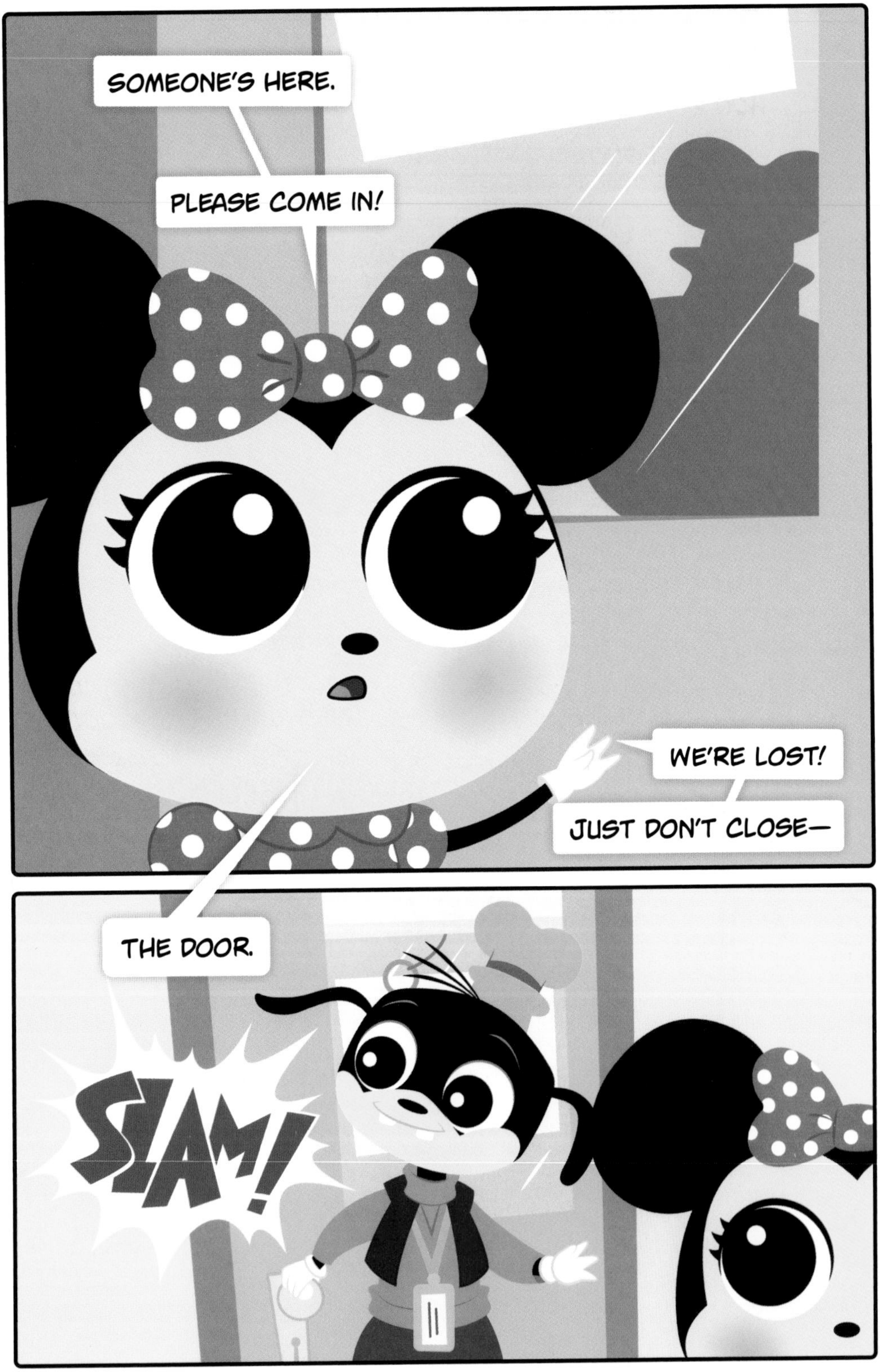
SOMEONE'S HERE.
PLEASE COME IN!
WE'RE LOST!
JUST DON'T CLOSE—
THE DOOR.
SLAM!

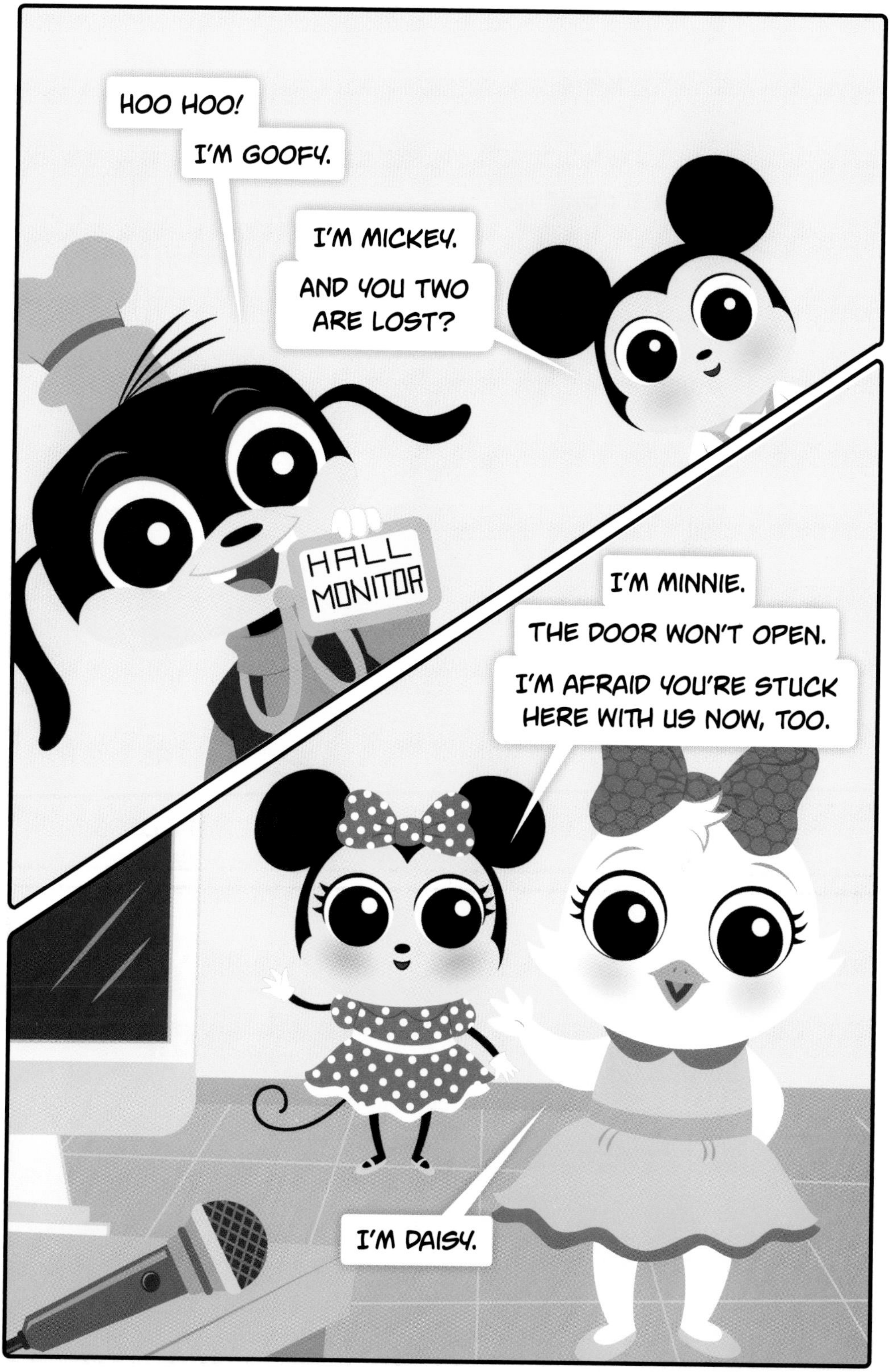
HOO HOO!
I'M GOOFY.
I'M MICKEY.
AND YOU TWO ARE LOST?
HALL MONITOR
I'M MINNIE.
THE DOOR WON'T OPEN.
I'M AFRAID YOU'RE STUCK HERE WITH US NOW, TOO.
I'M DAISY.

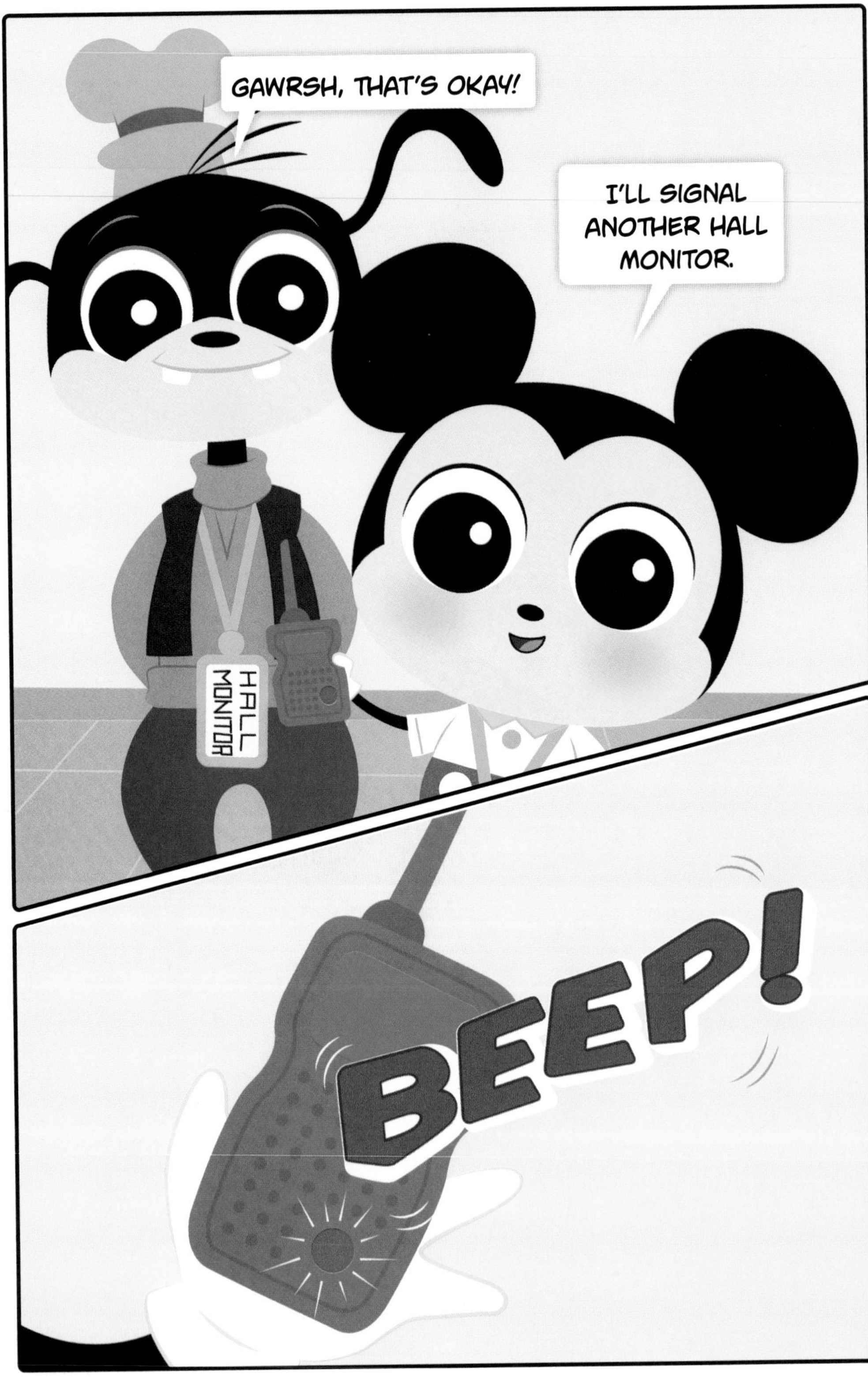
GAWRSH, THAT'S OKAY!
I'LL SIGNAL ANOTHER HALL MONITOR.
HALL MONITOR
BEEP!

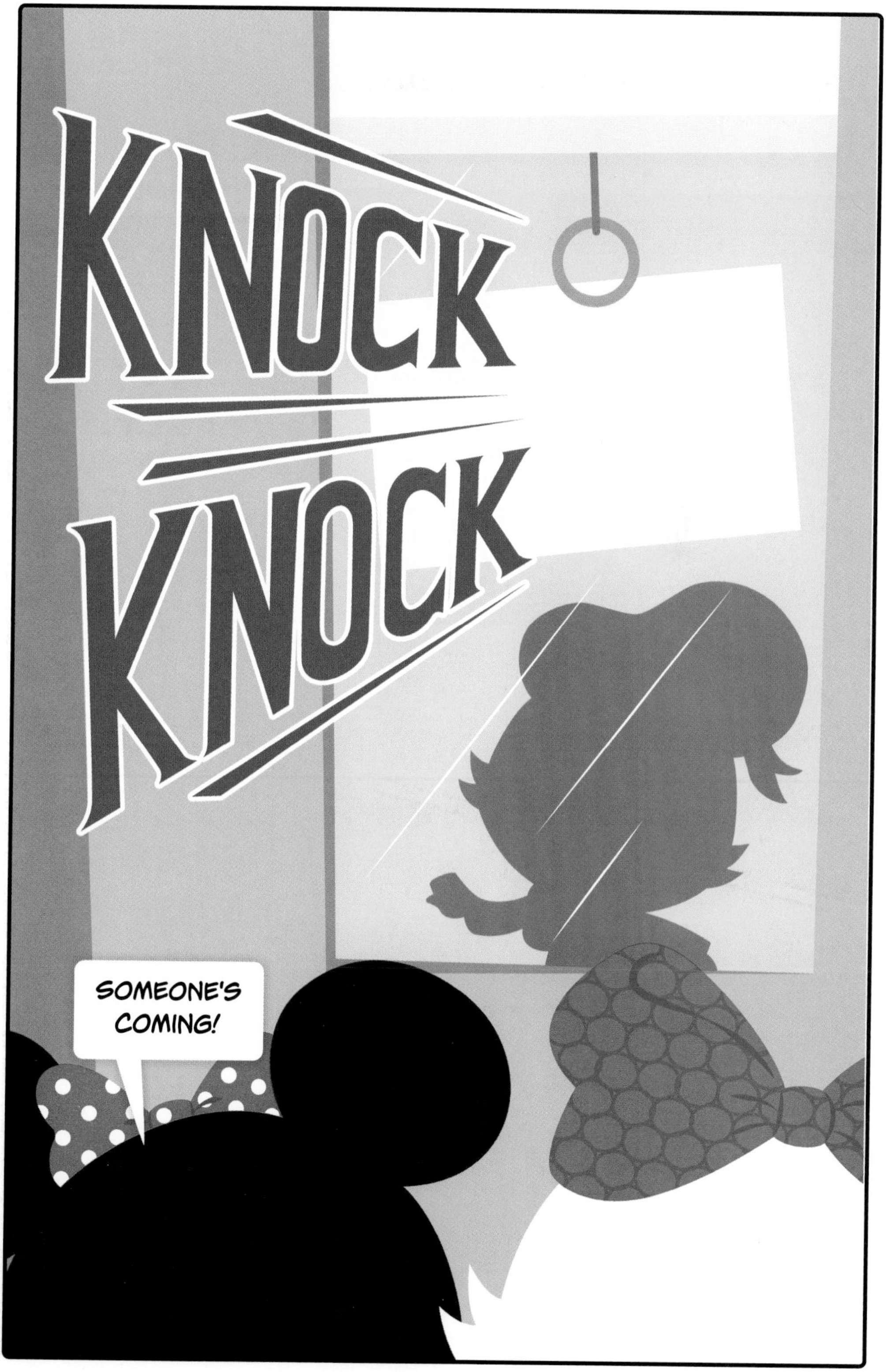
KNOCK
KNOCK
SOMEONE'S COMING!

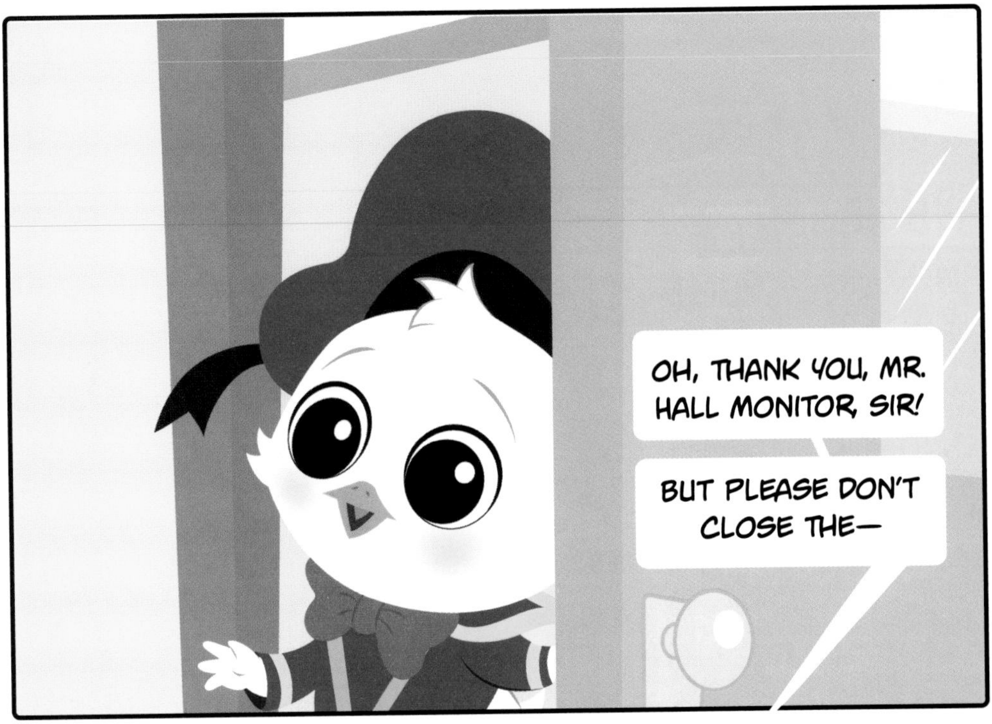
OH, THANK YOU, MR. HALL MONITOR, SIR!
BUT PLEASE DON'T CLOSE THE—

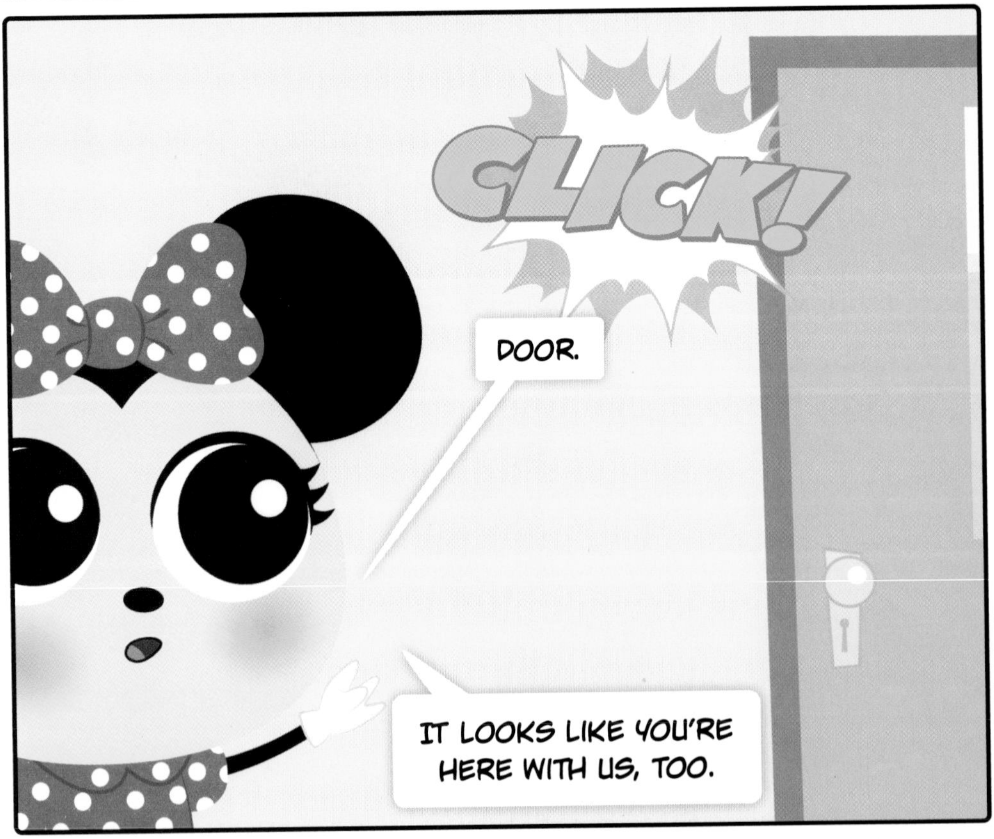
CLICK!
DOOR.
IT LOOKS LIKE YOU'RE HERE WITH US, TOO.

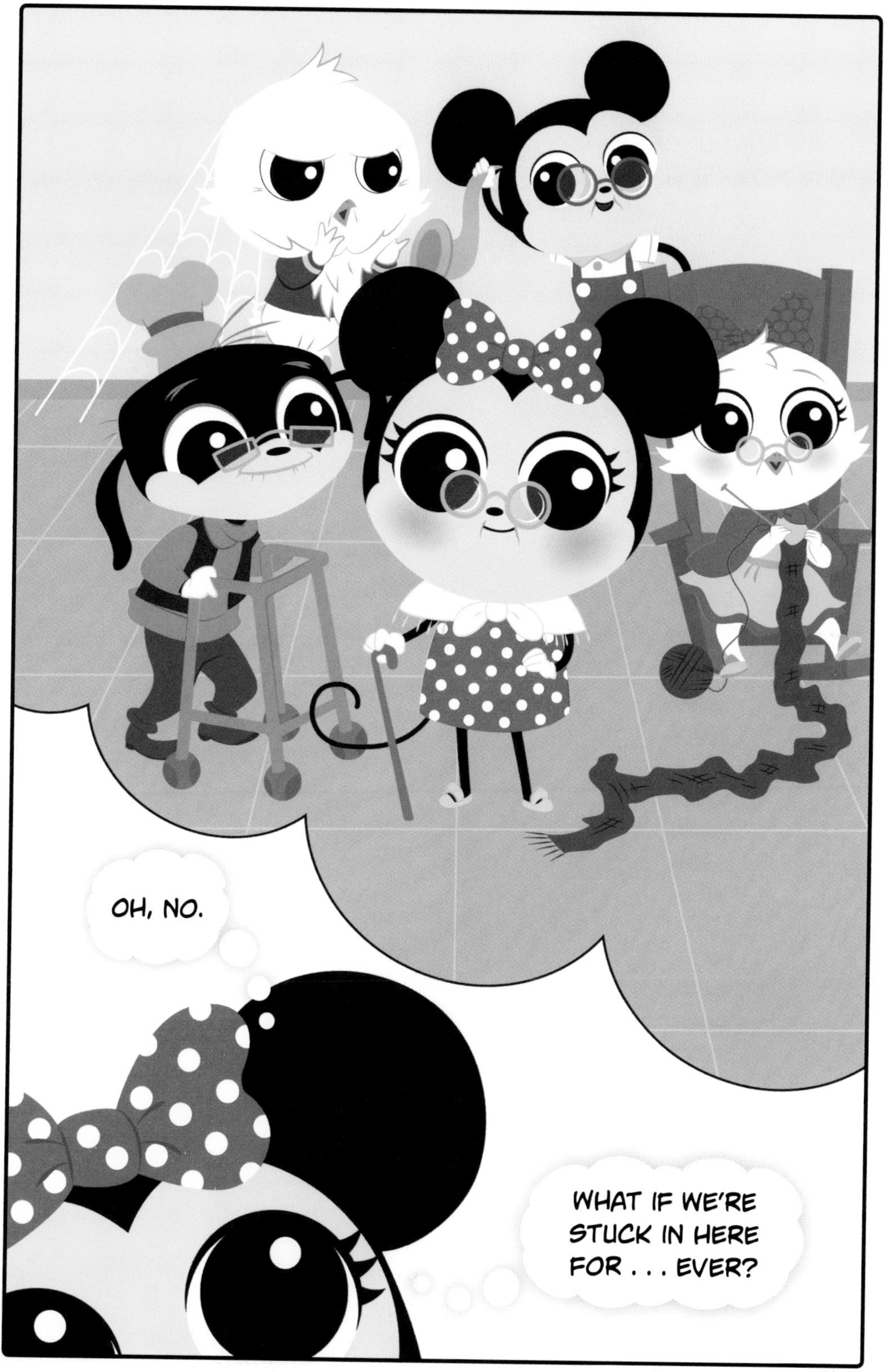
OH, NO.
WHAT IF WE'RE STUCK IN HERE FOR . . . EVER?

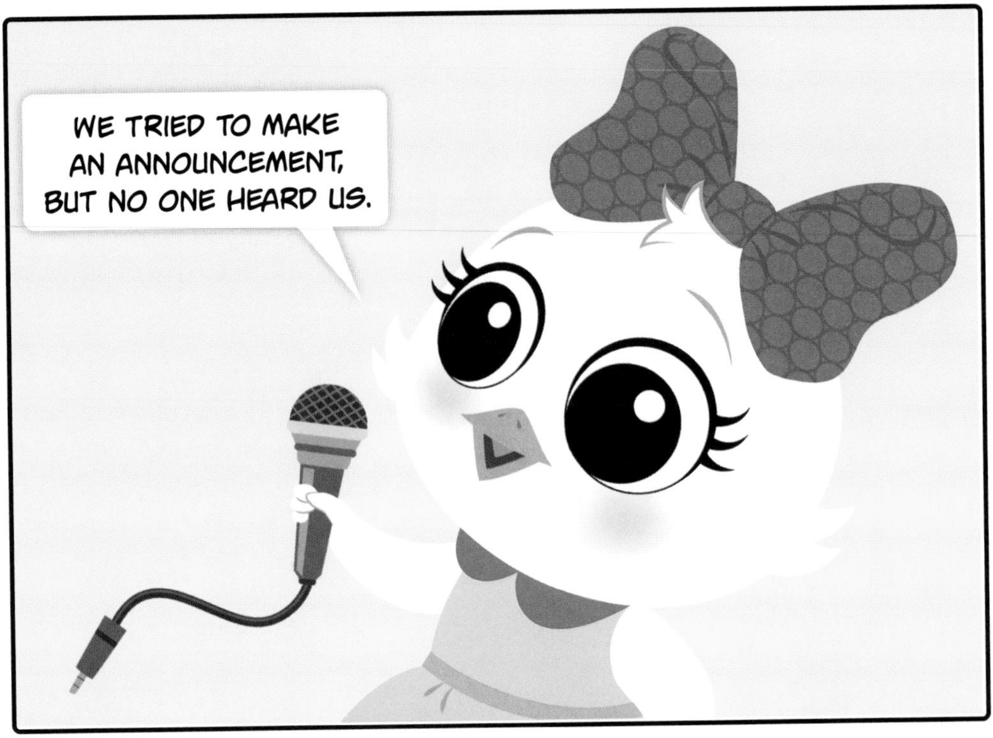
WE TRIED TO MAKE AN ANNOUNCEMENT, BUT NO ONE HEARD US.

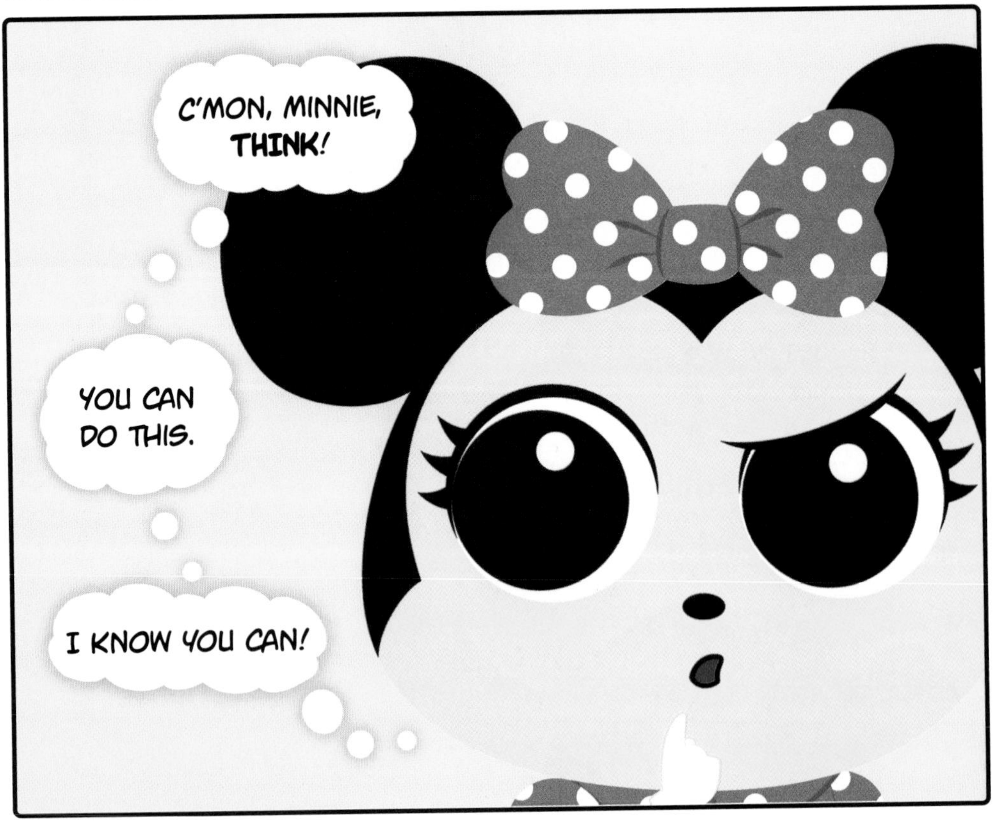
C'MON, MINNIE, THINK!
YOU CAN DO THIS.
I KNOW YOU CAN!

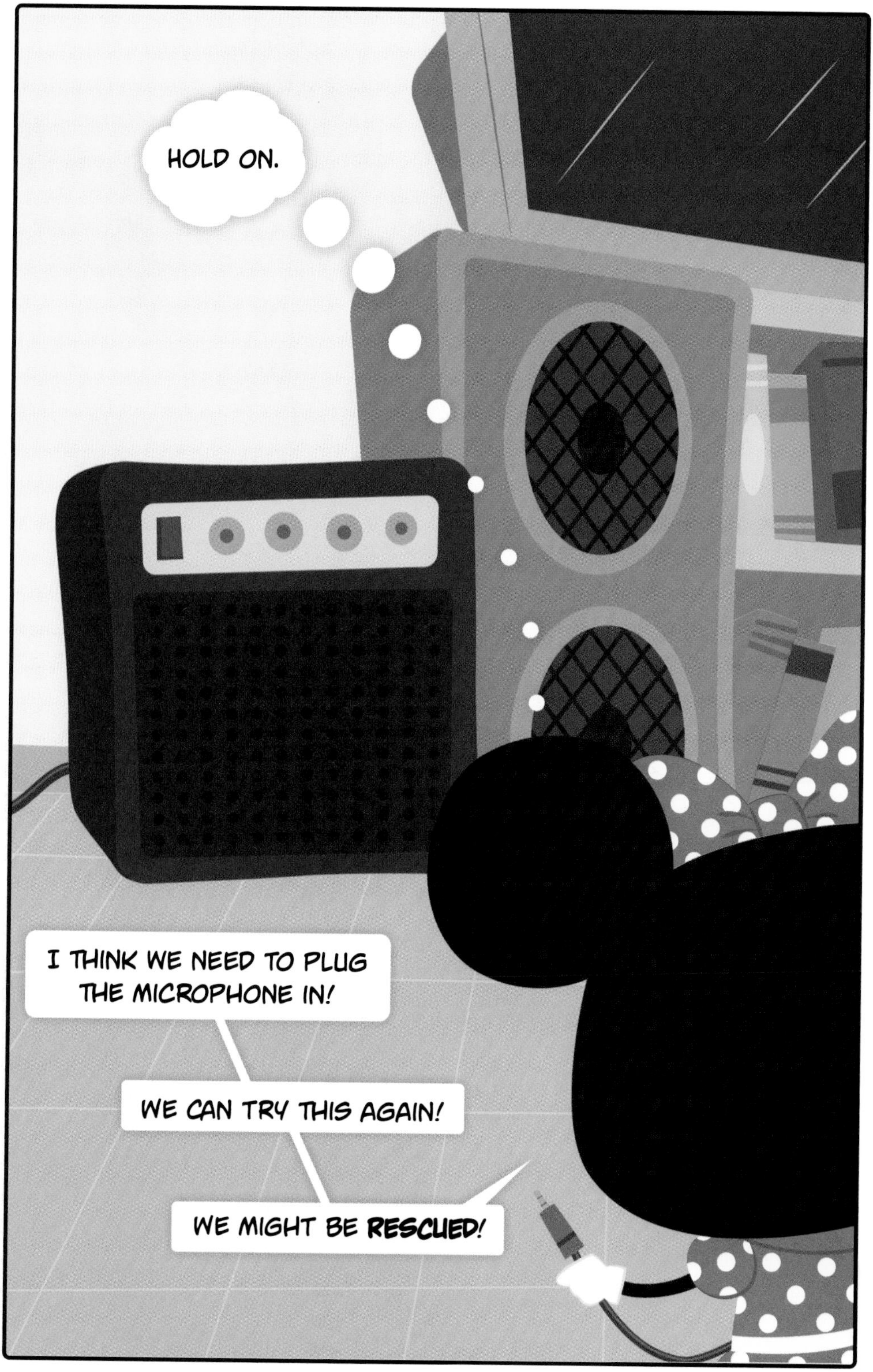
HOLD ON.
I THINK WE NEED TO PLUG THE MICROPHONE IN!
WE CAN TRY THIS AGAIN!
WE MIGHT BE **RESCUED!**

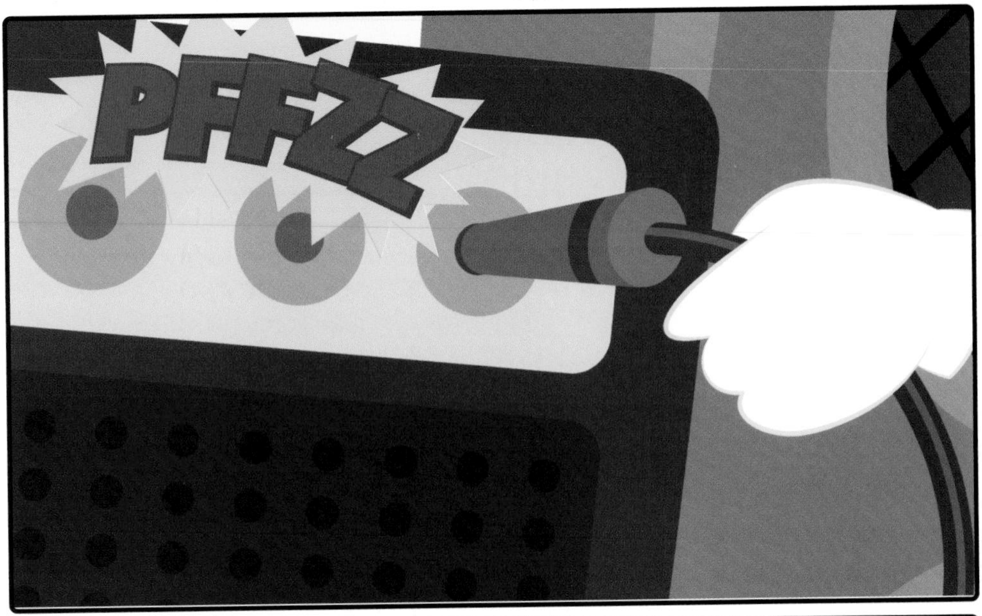
PFFZZ

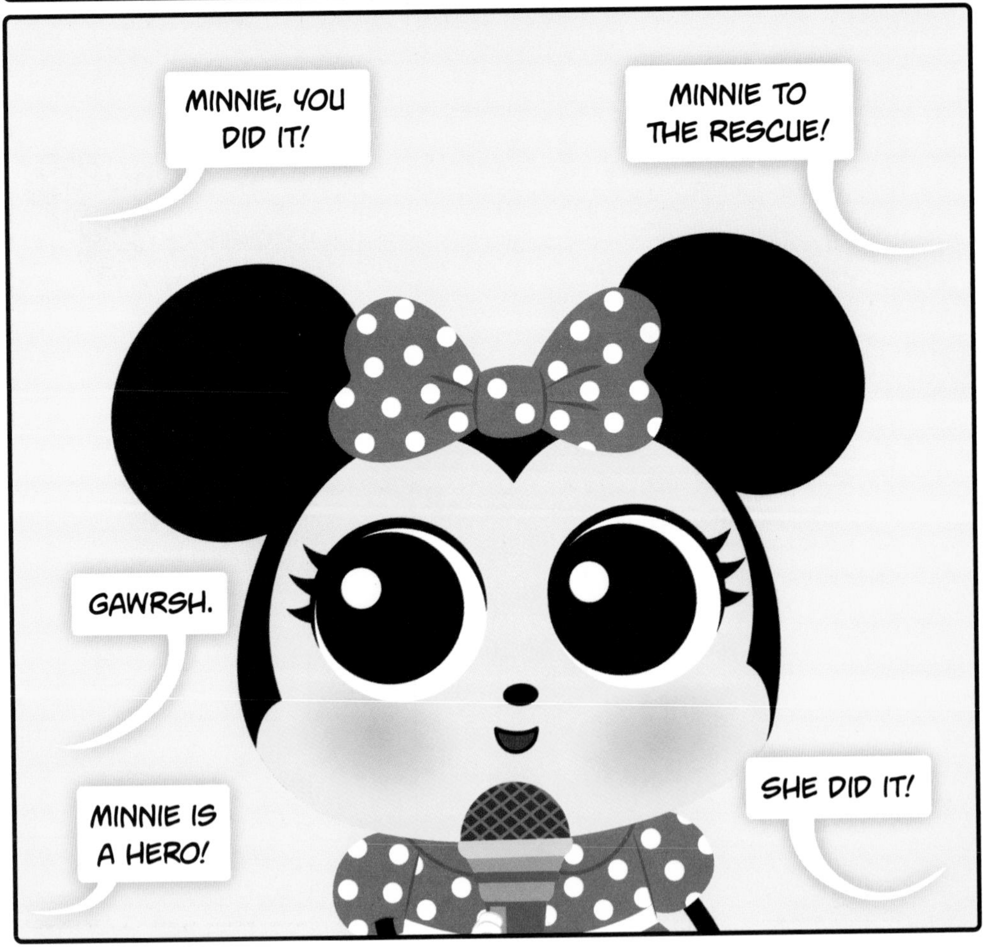
MINNIE, YOU DID IT!
MINNIE TO THE RESCUE!
GAWRSH.
MINNIE IS A HERO!
SHE DID IT!

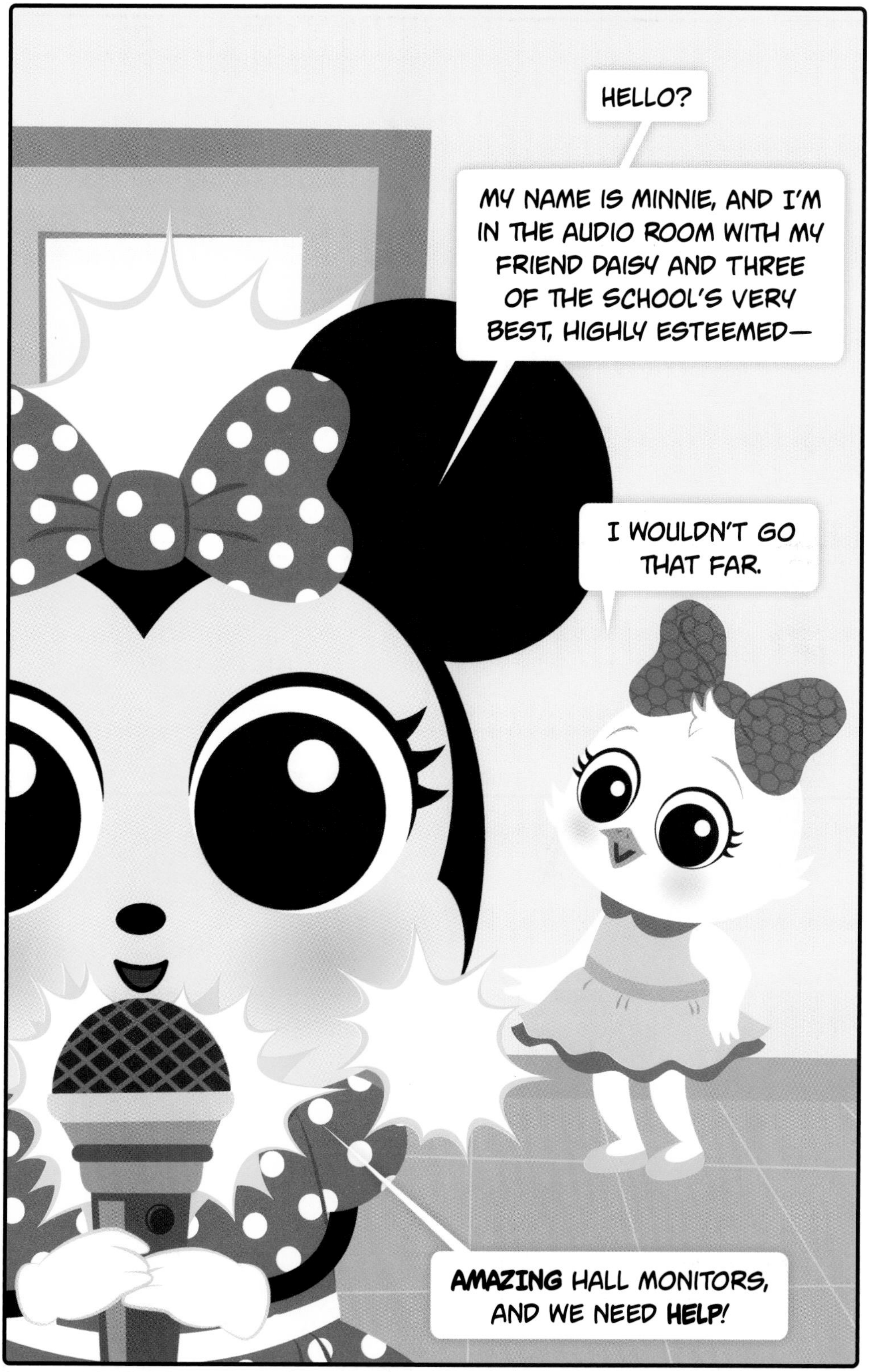
HELLO?
MY NAME IS MINNIE, AND I'M IN THE AUDIO ROOM WITH MY FRIEND DAISY AND THREE OF THE SCHOOL'S VERY BEST, HIGHLY ESTEEMED—
I WOULDN'T GO THAT FAR.
AMAZING HALL MONITORS, AND WE NEED **HELP**!

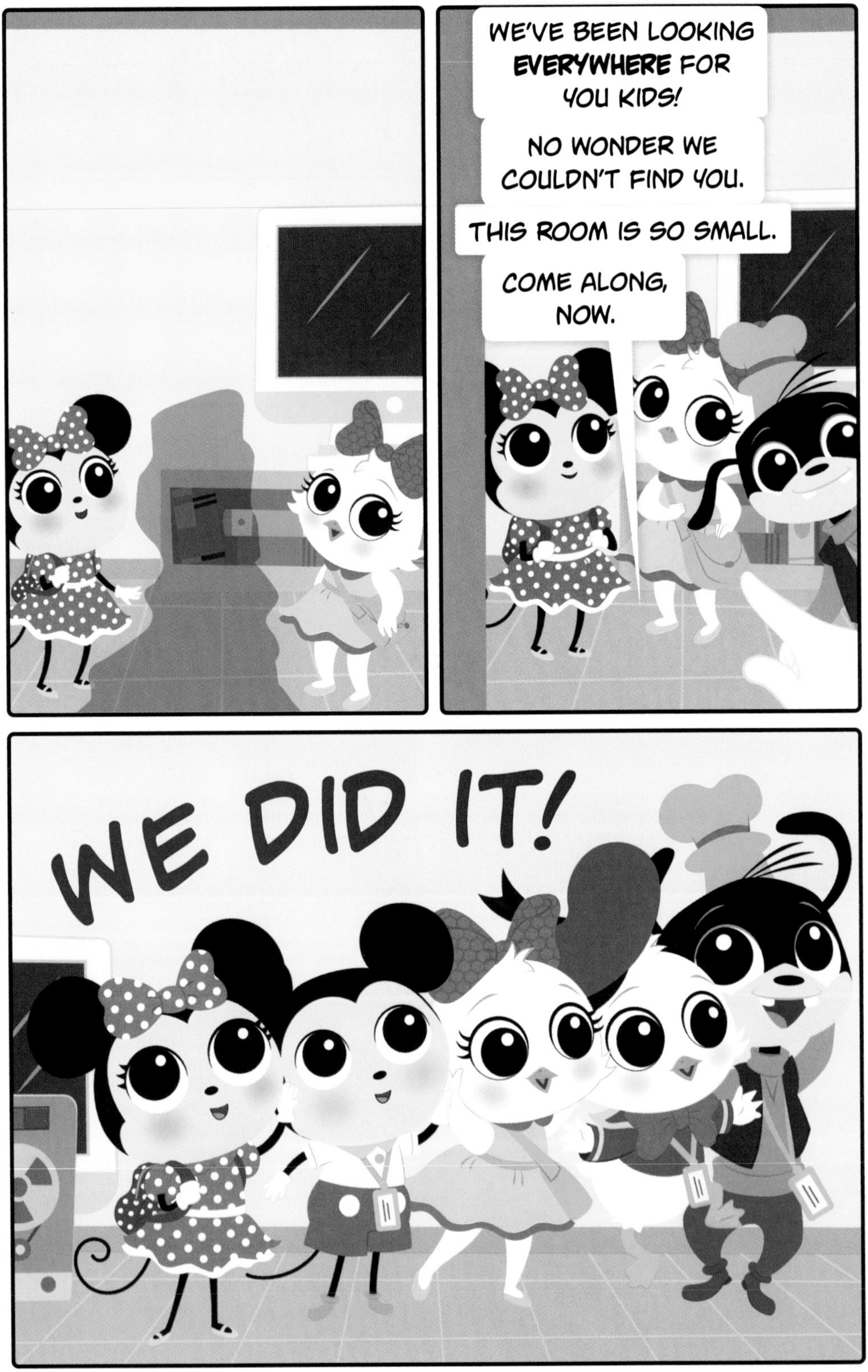
WE'VE BEEN LOOKING **EVERYWHERE** FOR YOU KIDS!
NO WONDER WE COULDN'T FIND YOU.
THIS ROOM IS SO SMALL.
COME ALONG, NOW.
WE DID IT!

PART 2

RECESS TIME!

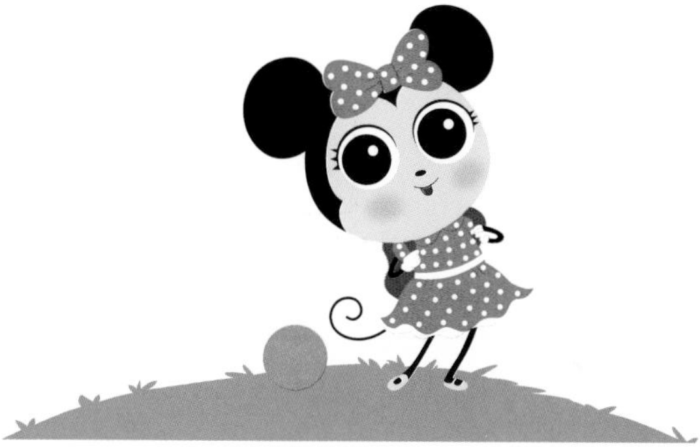

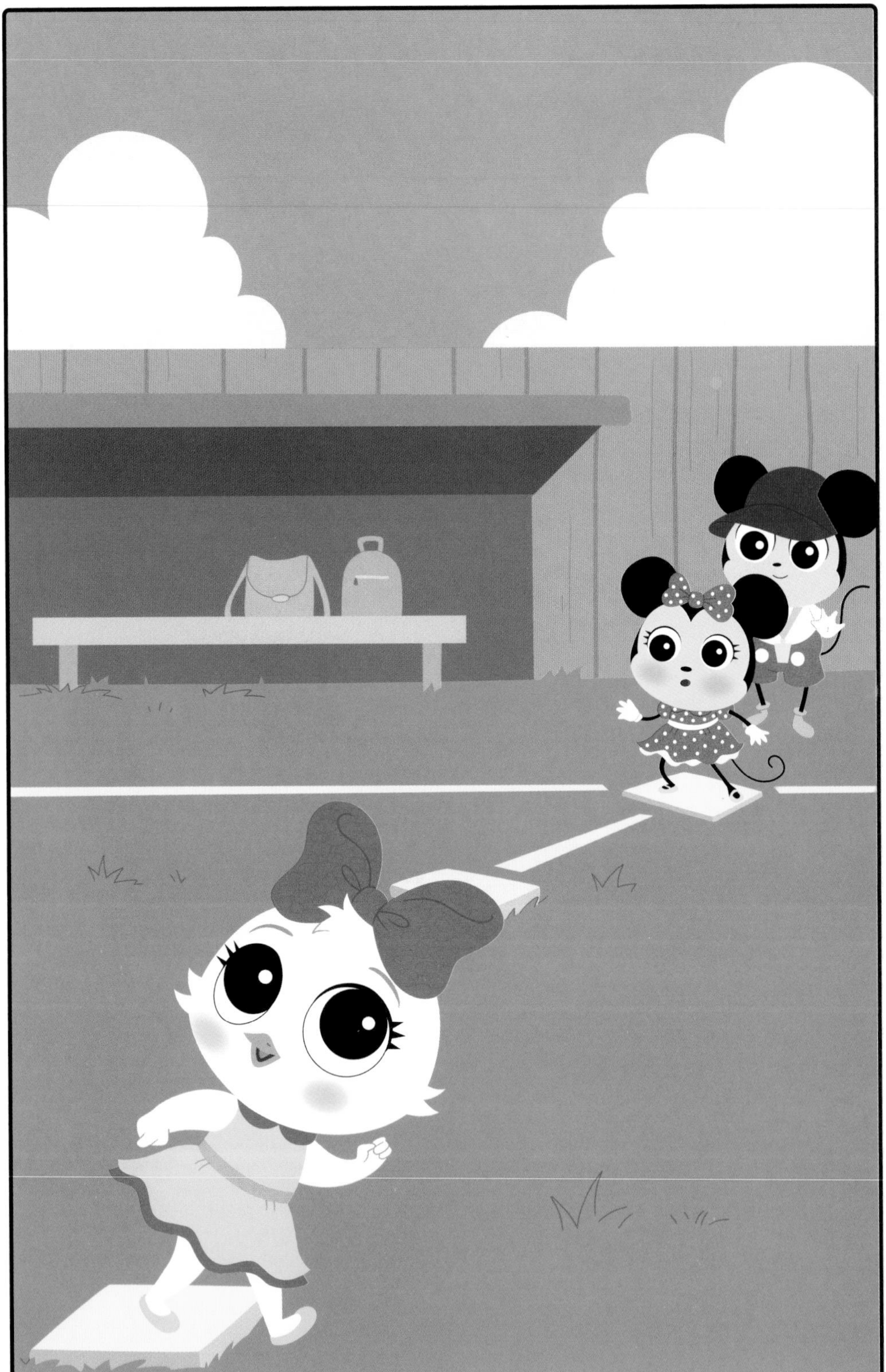

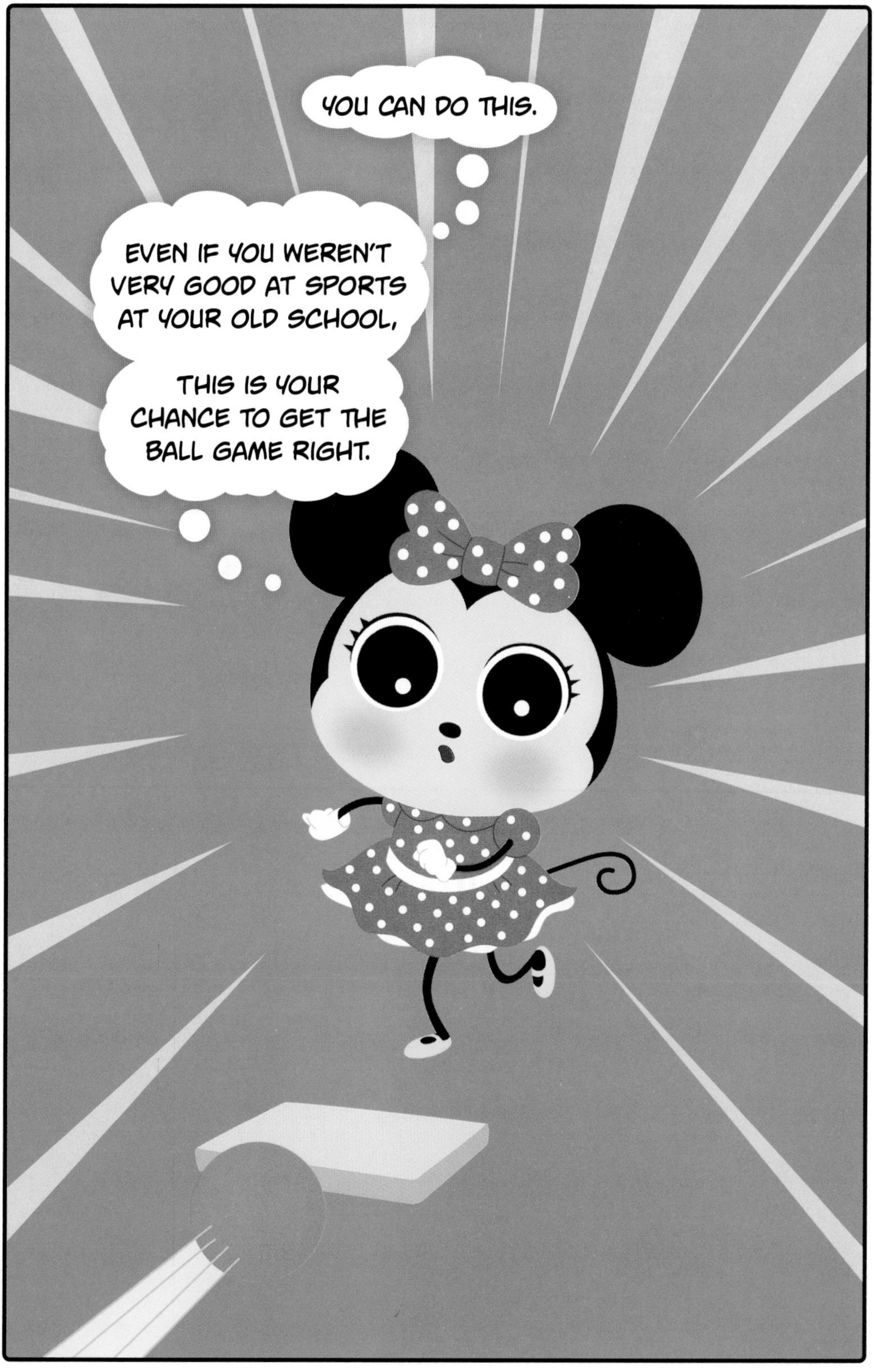
YOU CAN DO THIS.
EVEN IF YOU WEREN'T VERY GOOD AT SPORTS AT YOUR OLD SCHOOL,
THIS IS YOUR CHANCE TO GET THE BALL GAME RIGHT.

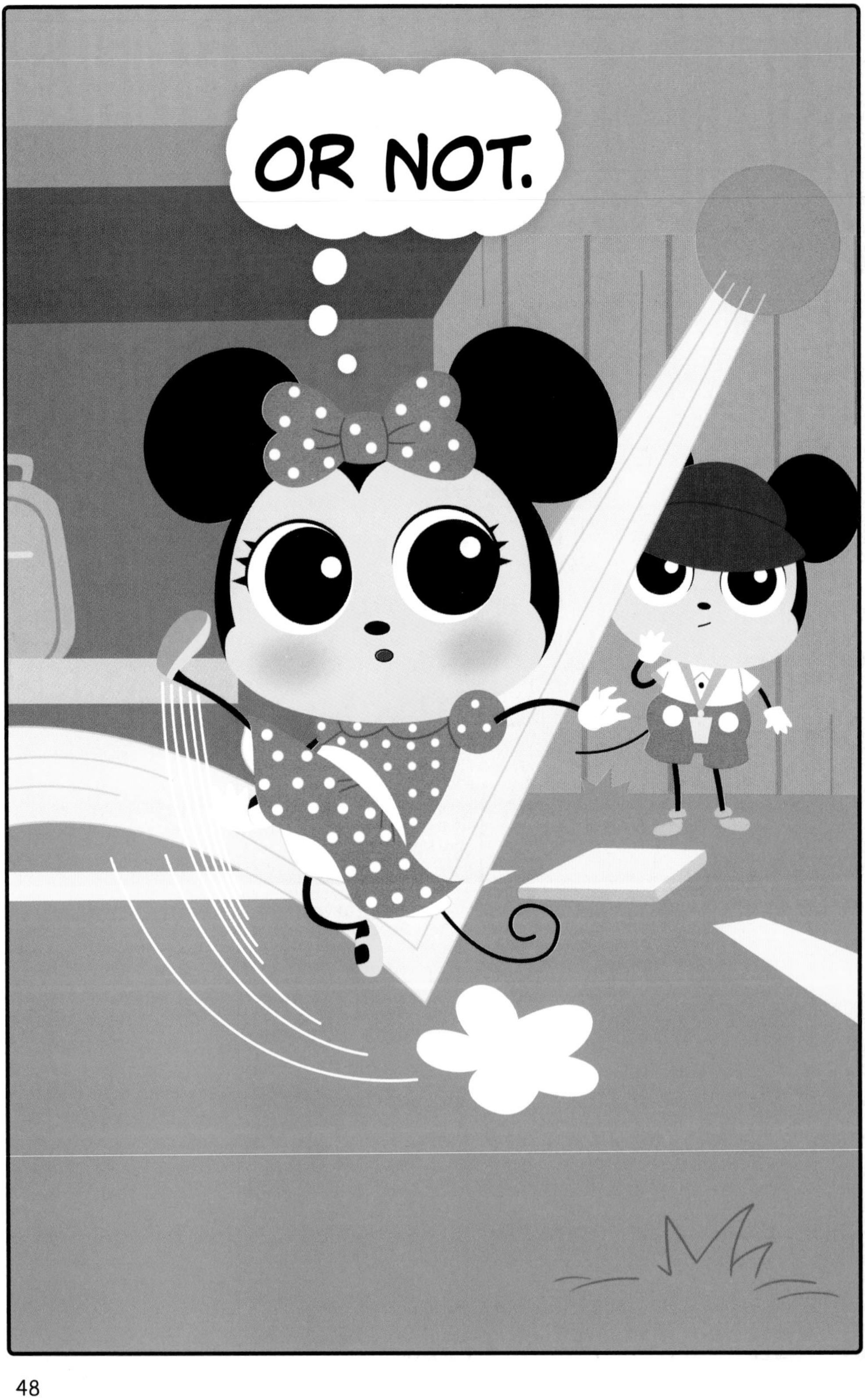
OR NOT.

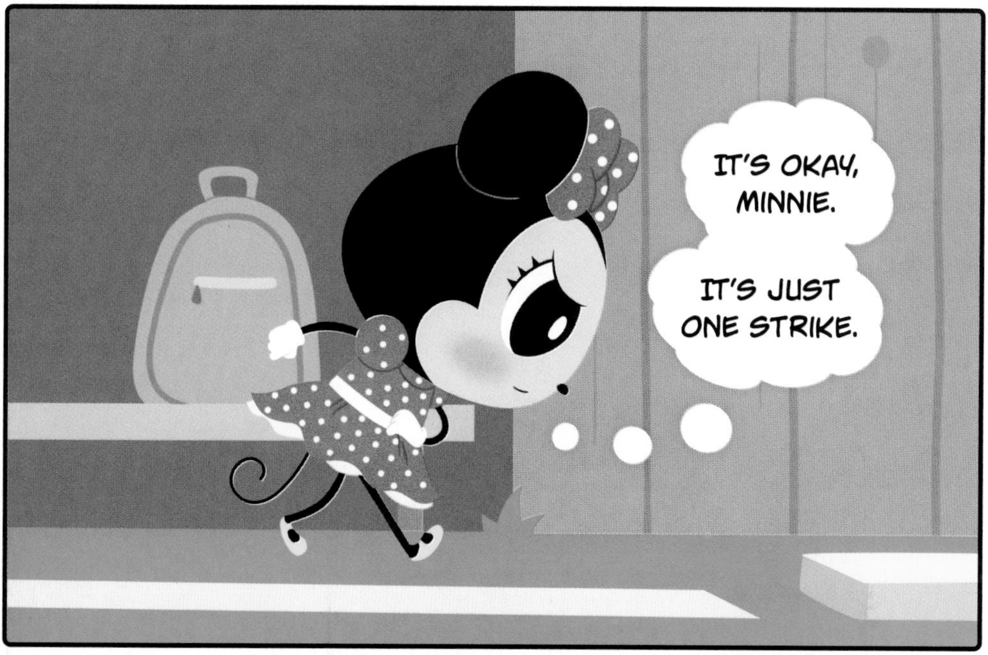
IT'S OKAY, MINNIE.
IT'S JUST ONE STRIKE.

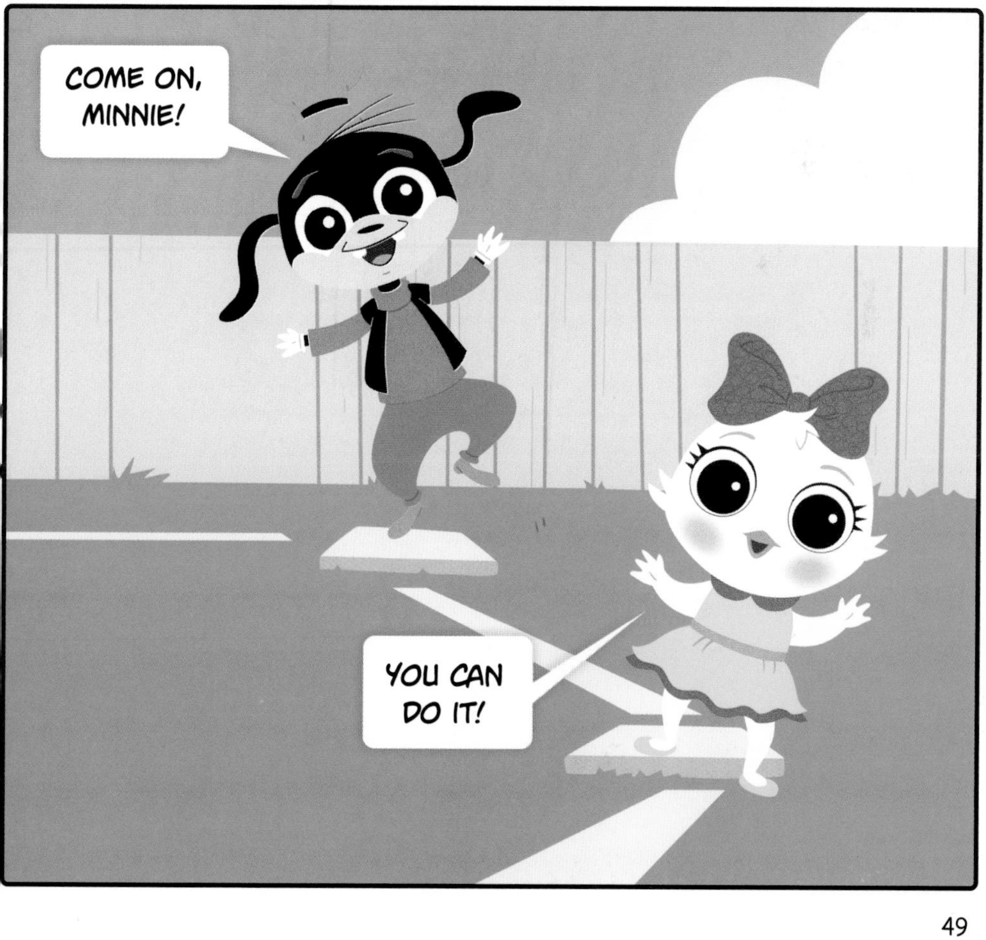
COME ON, MINNIE!
YOU CAN DO IT!

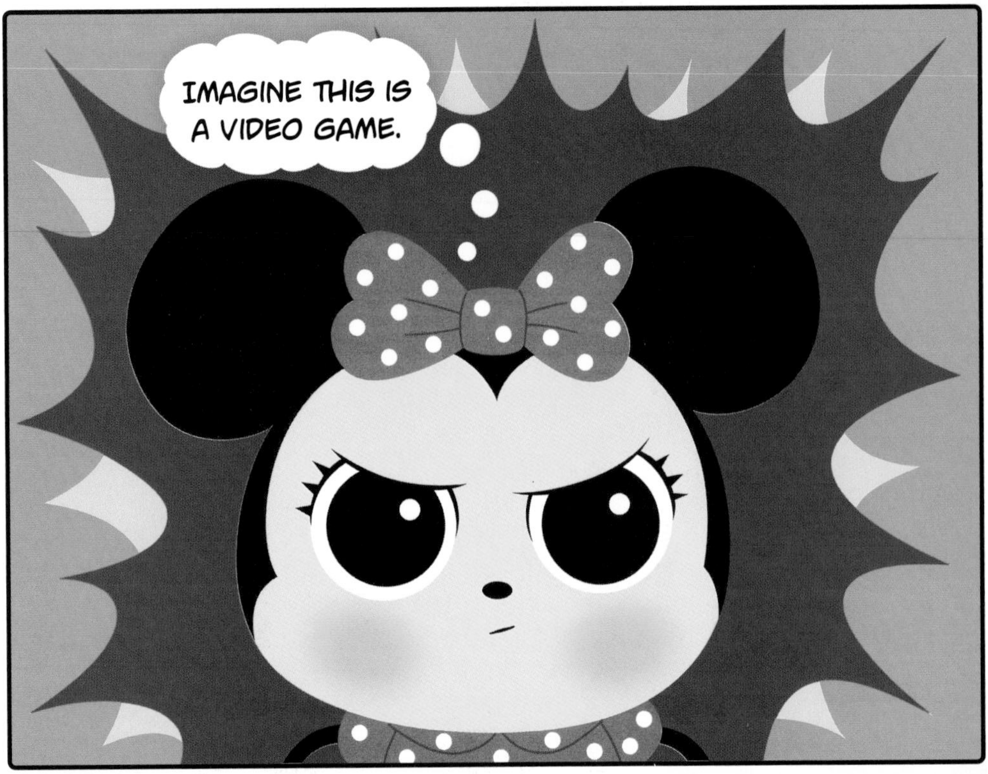
IMAGINE THIS IS A VIDEO GAME.

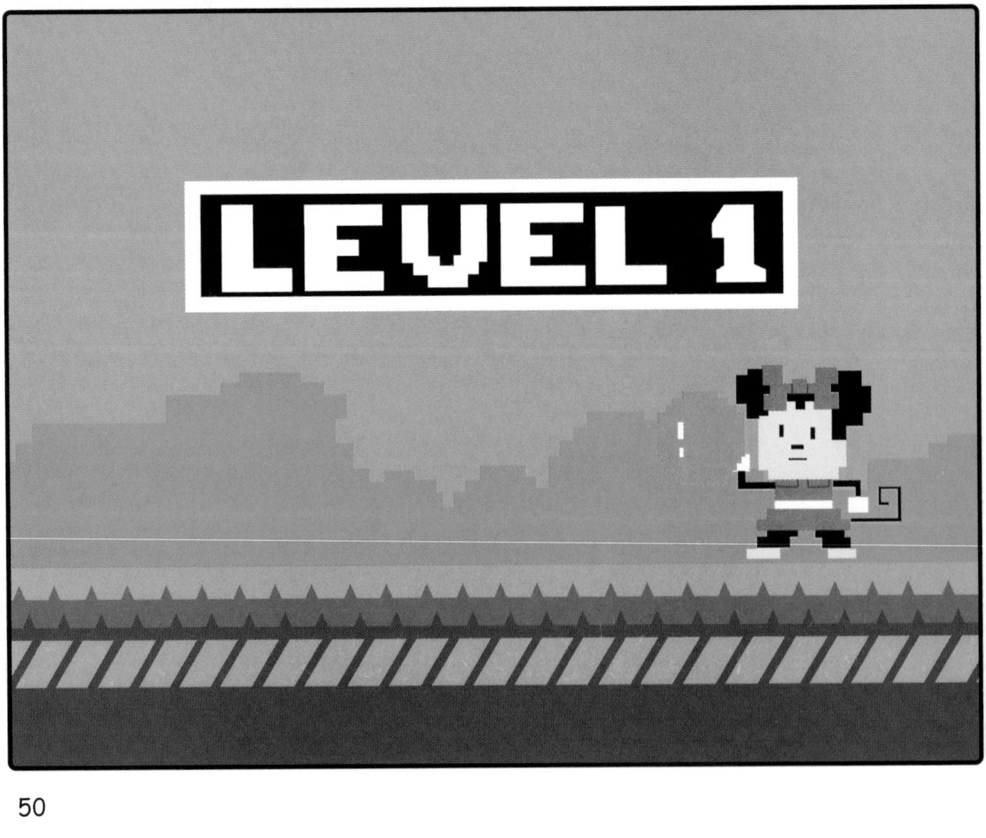
LEVEL 1

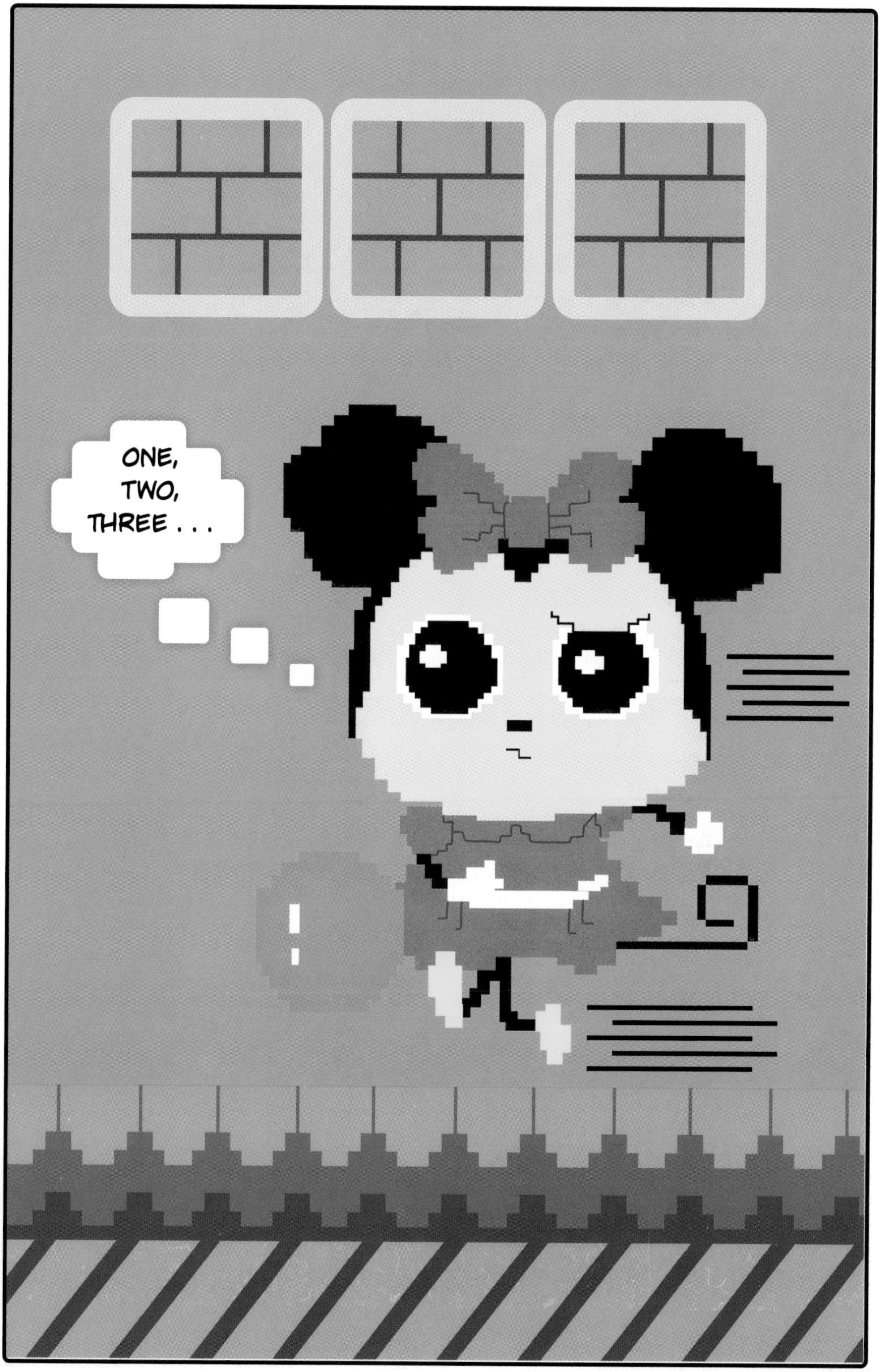
ONE, TWO, THREE . . .

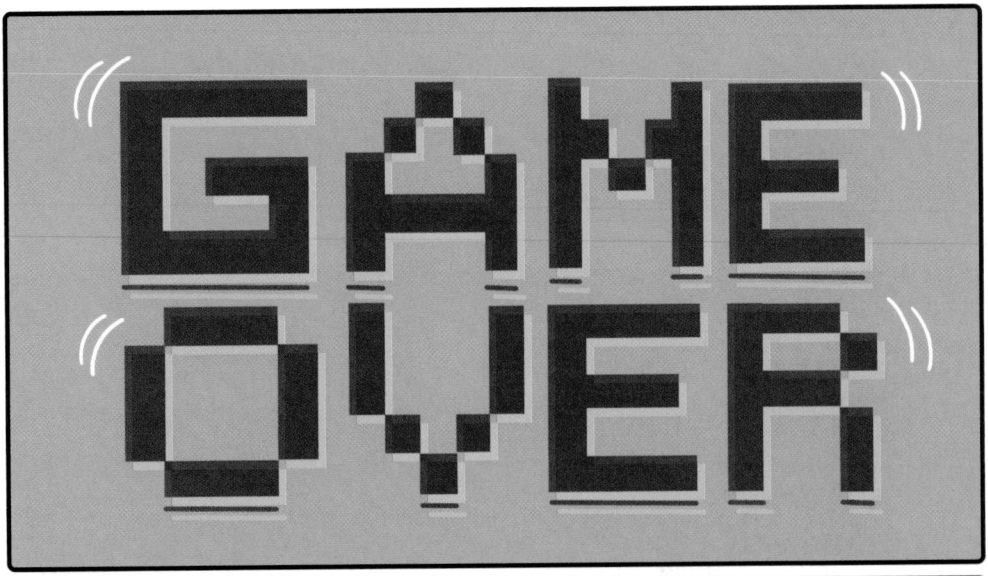
GAME OVER

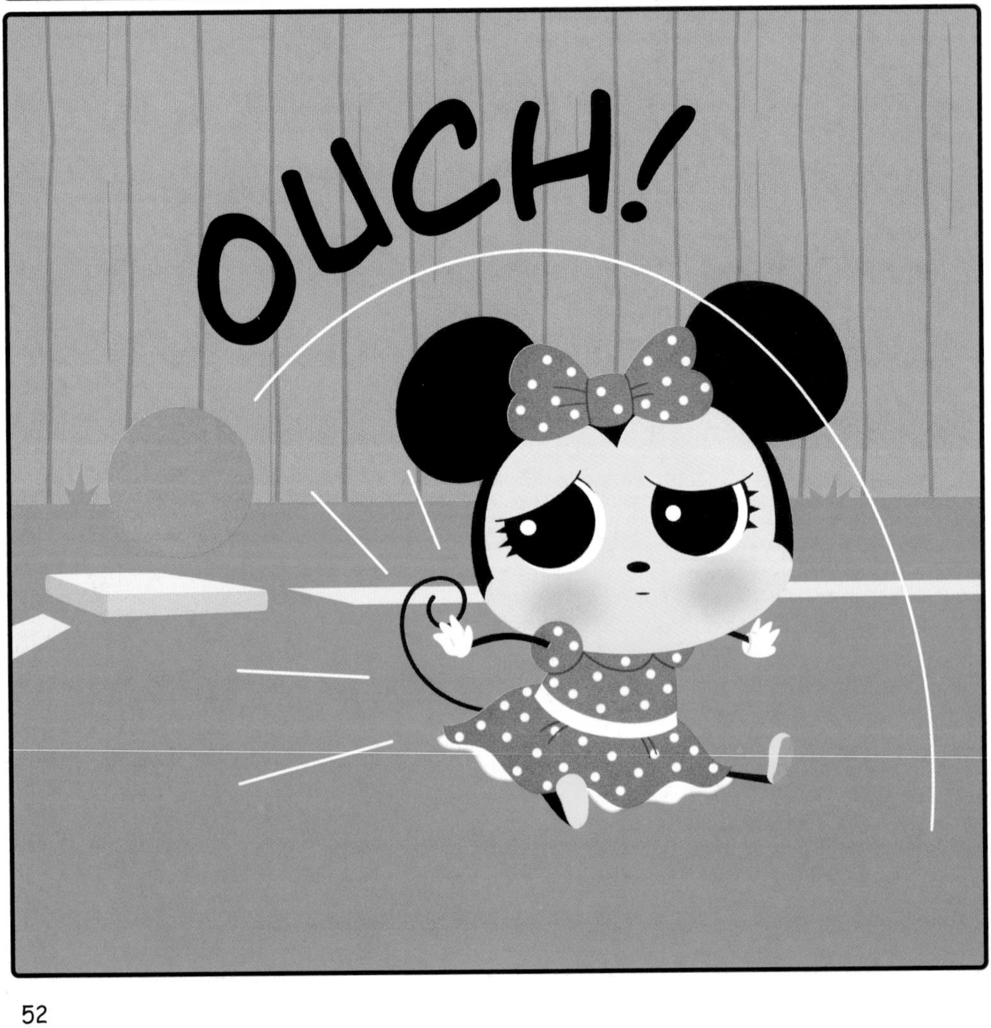
OUCH!

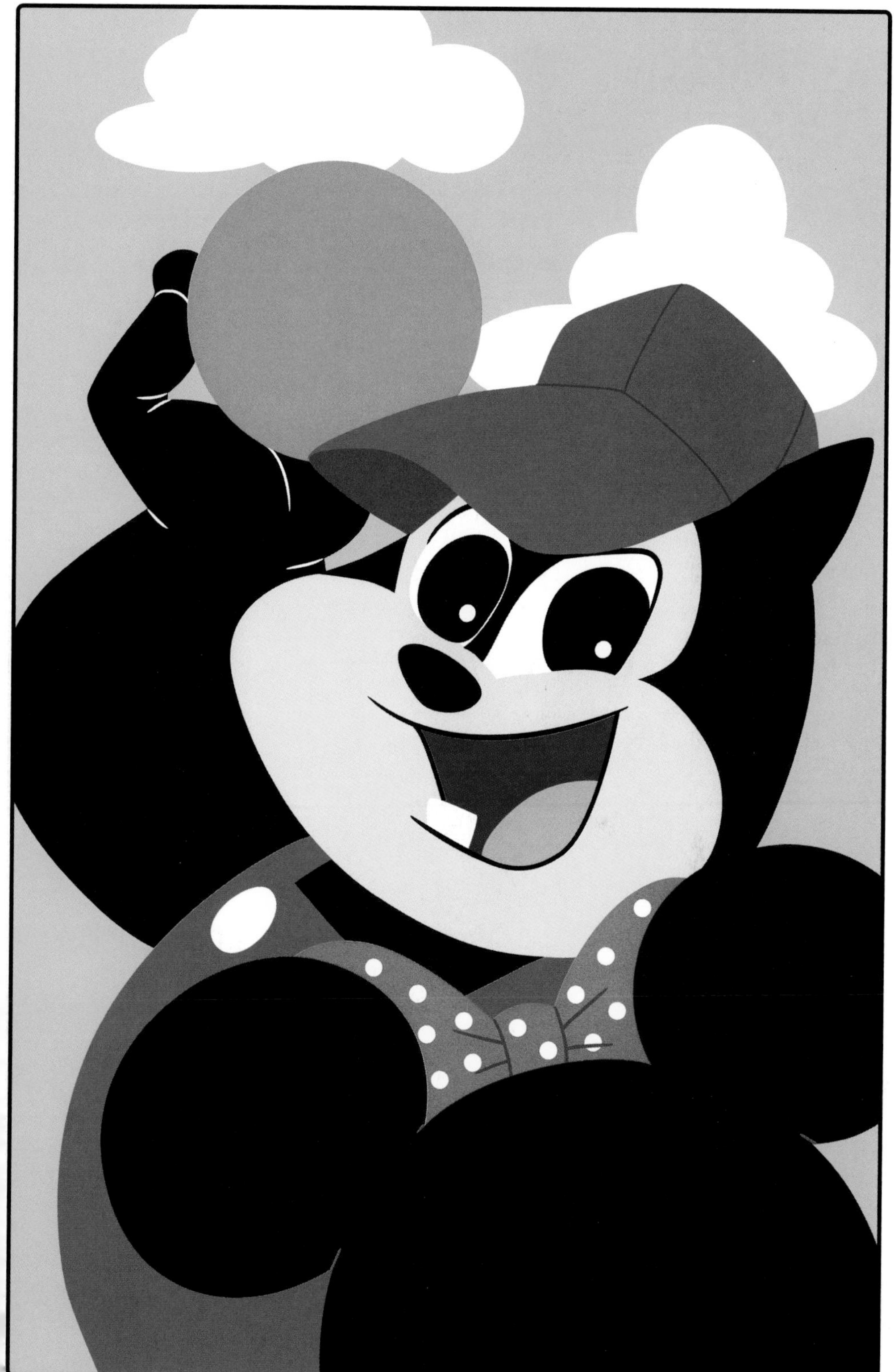

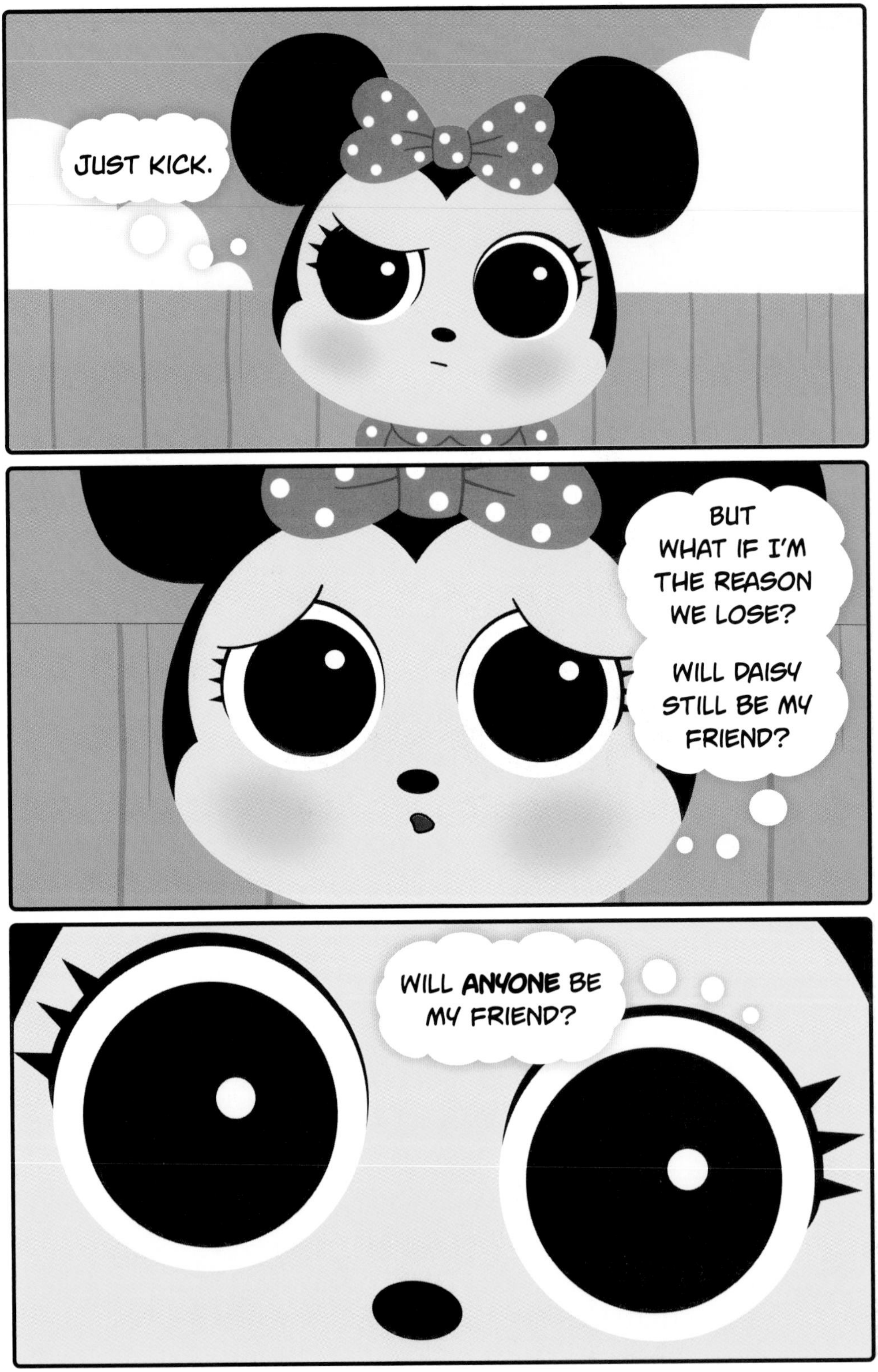
JUST KICK.
BUT WHAT IF I'M THE REASON WE LOSE?
WILL DAISY STILL BE MY FRIEND?
WILL ANYONE BE MY FRIEND?

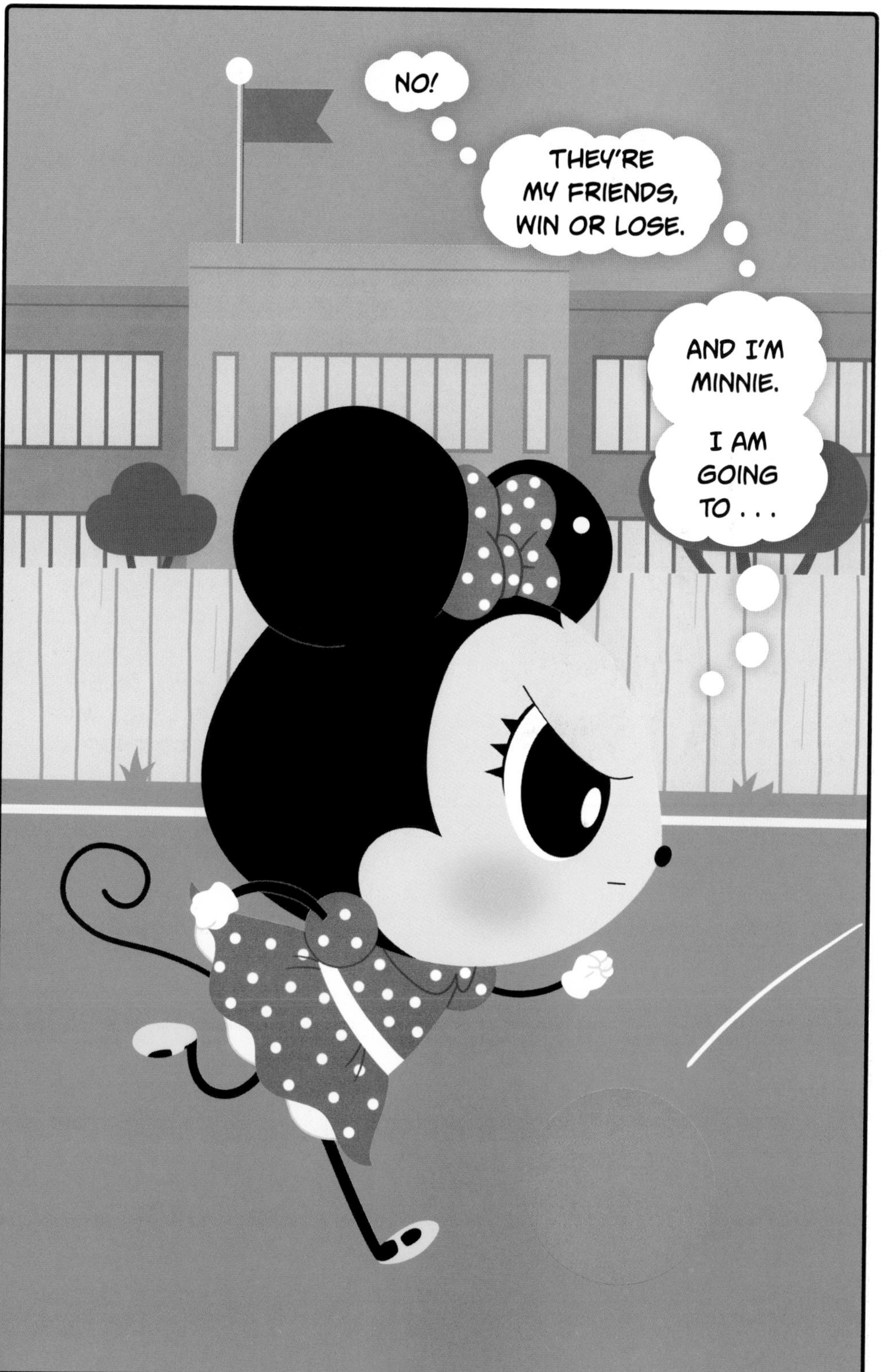
NO!
THEY'RE MY FRIENDS, WIN OR LOSE.
AND I'M MINNIE.
I AM GOING TO . . .

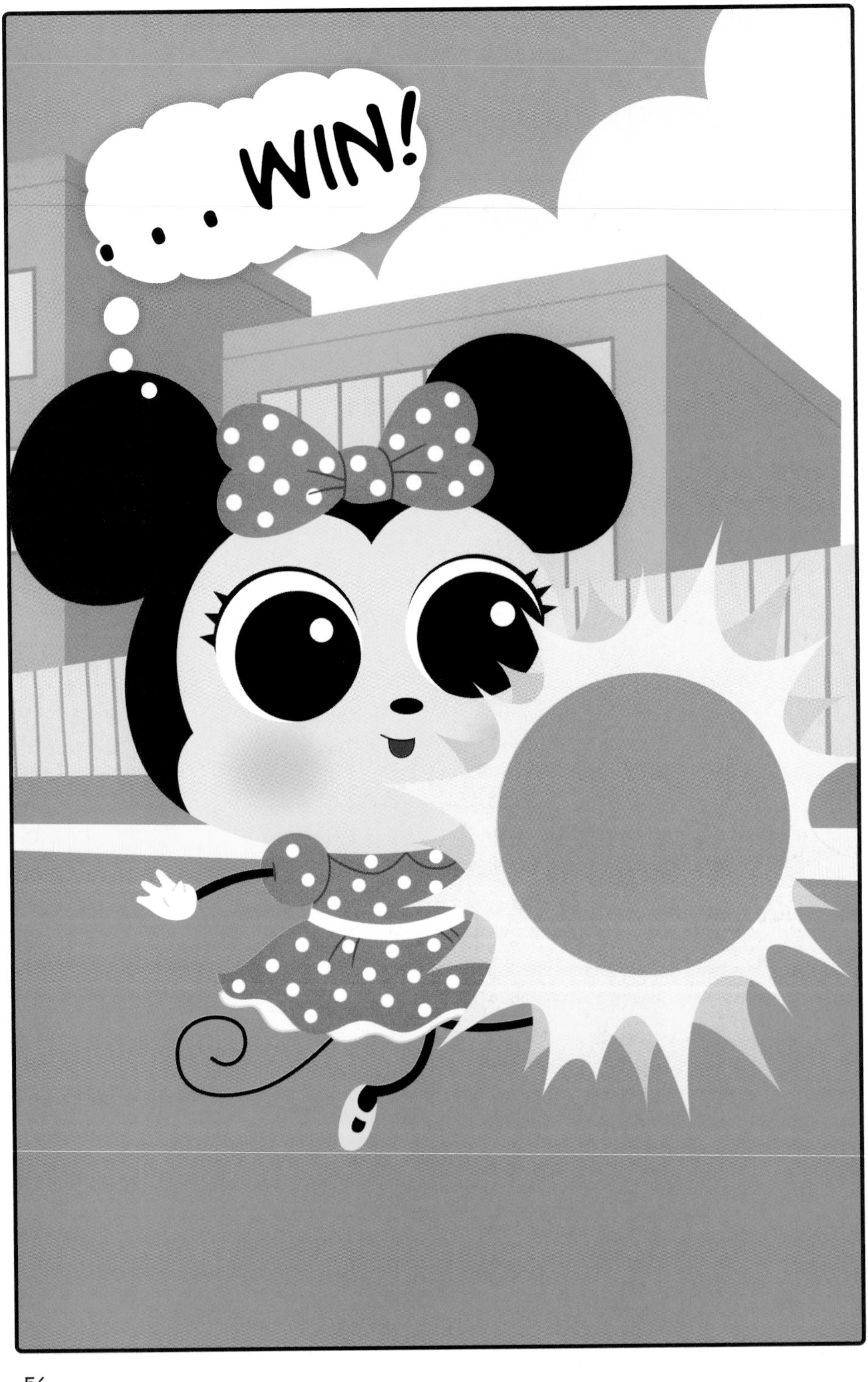
. . . WIN!

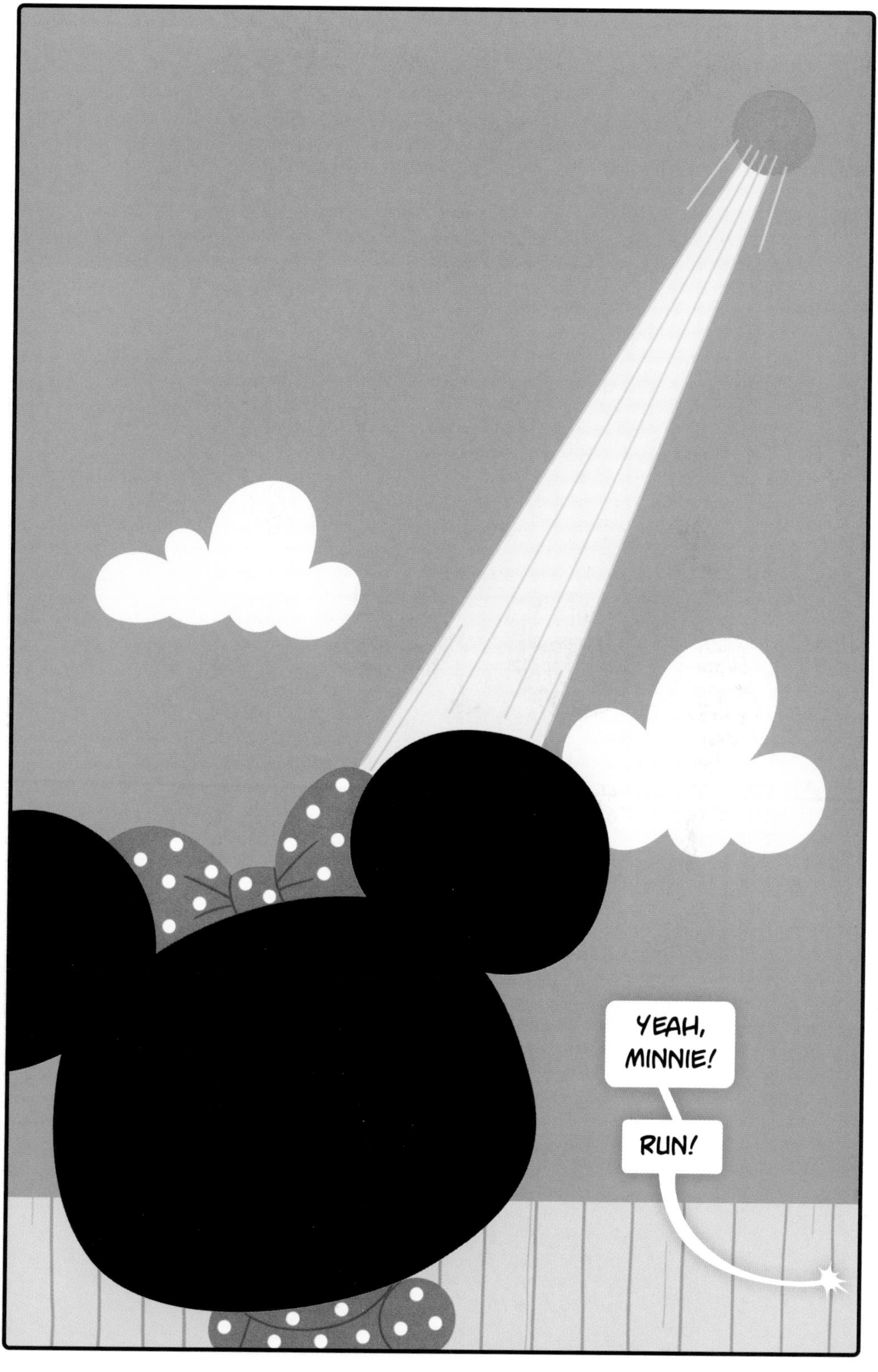
YEAH, MINNIE!
RUN!

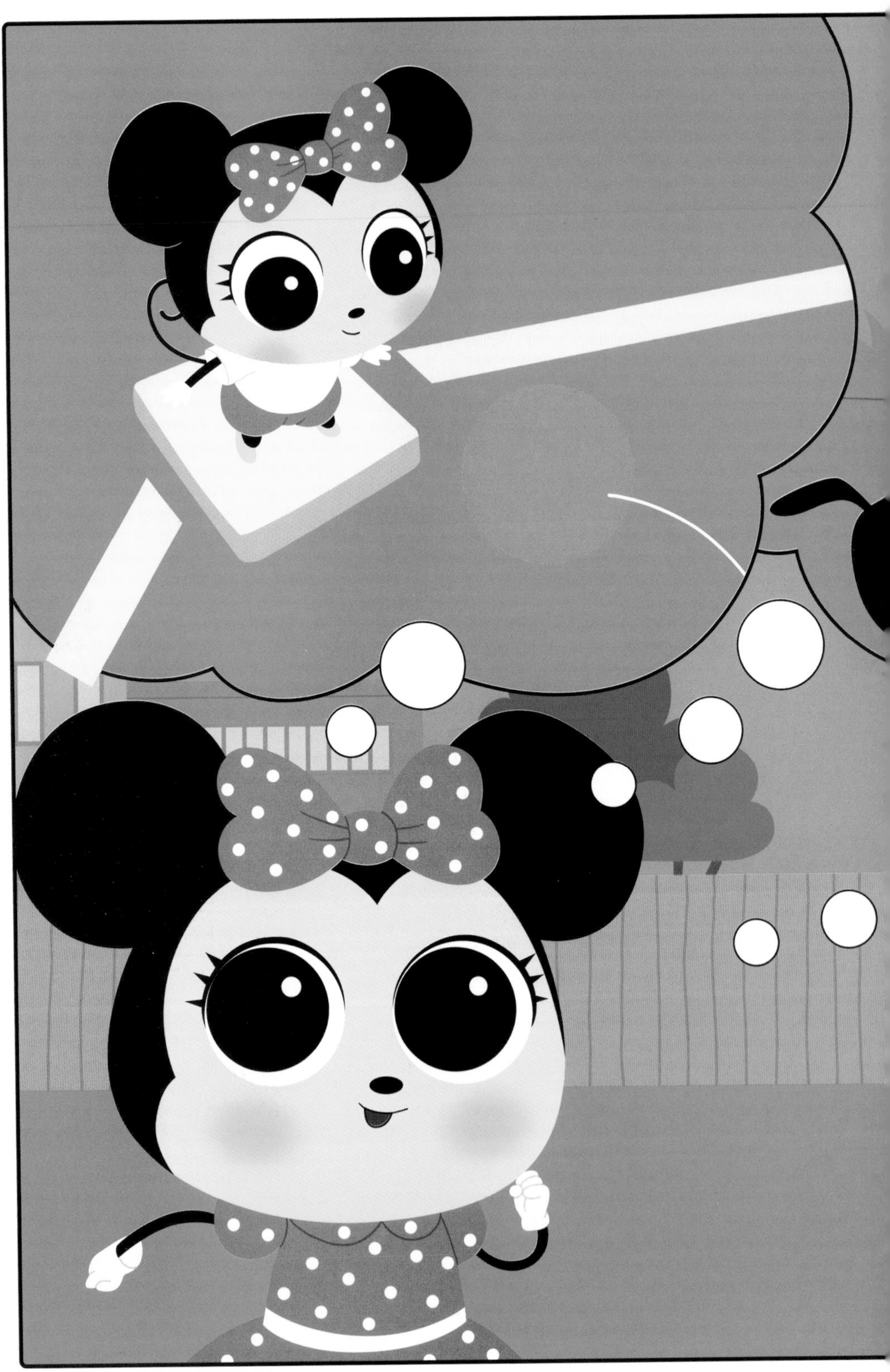

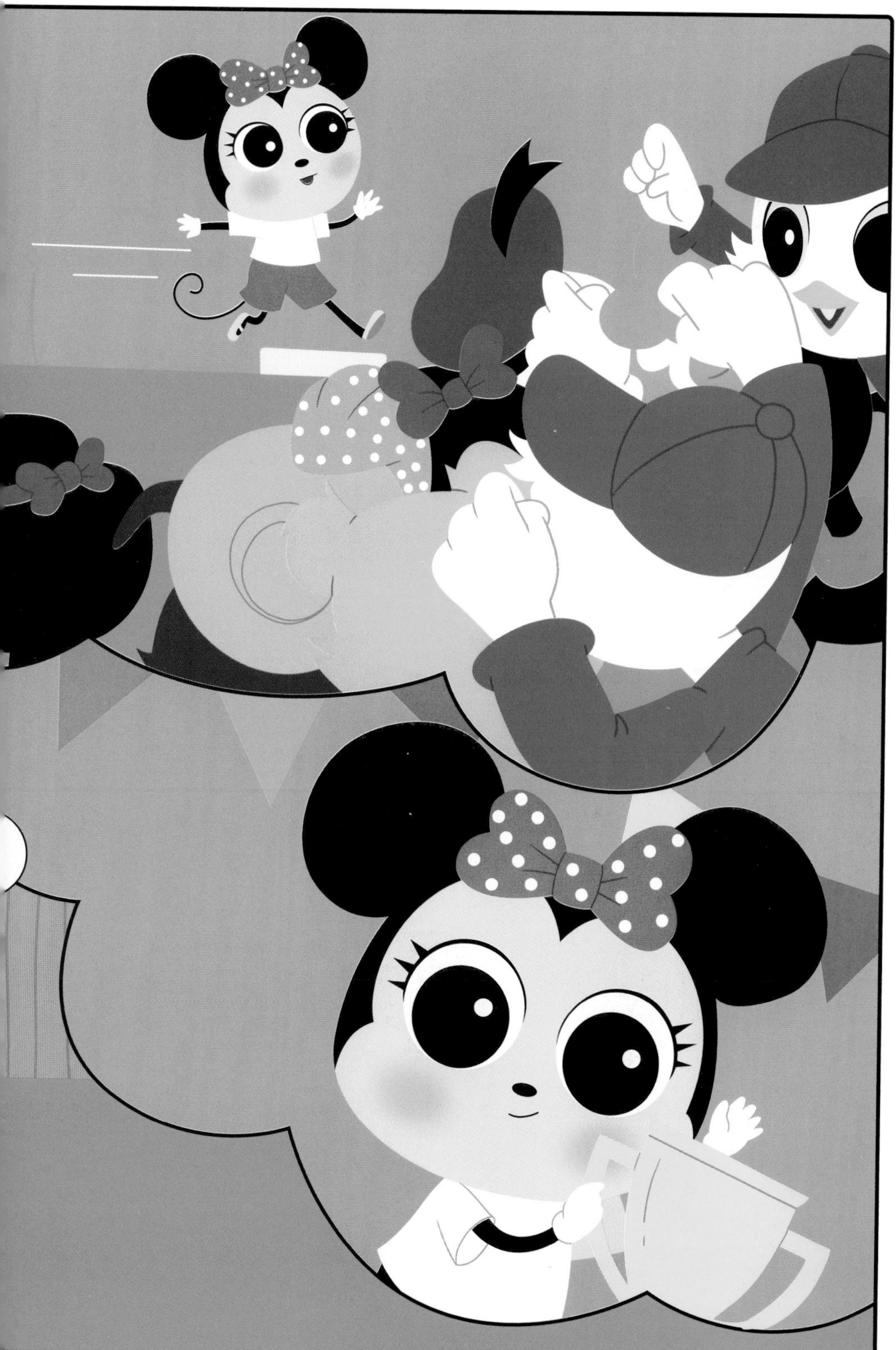

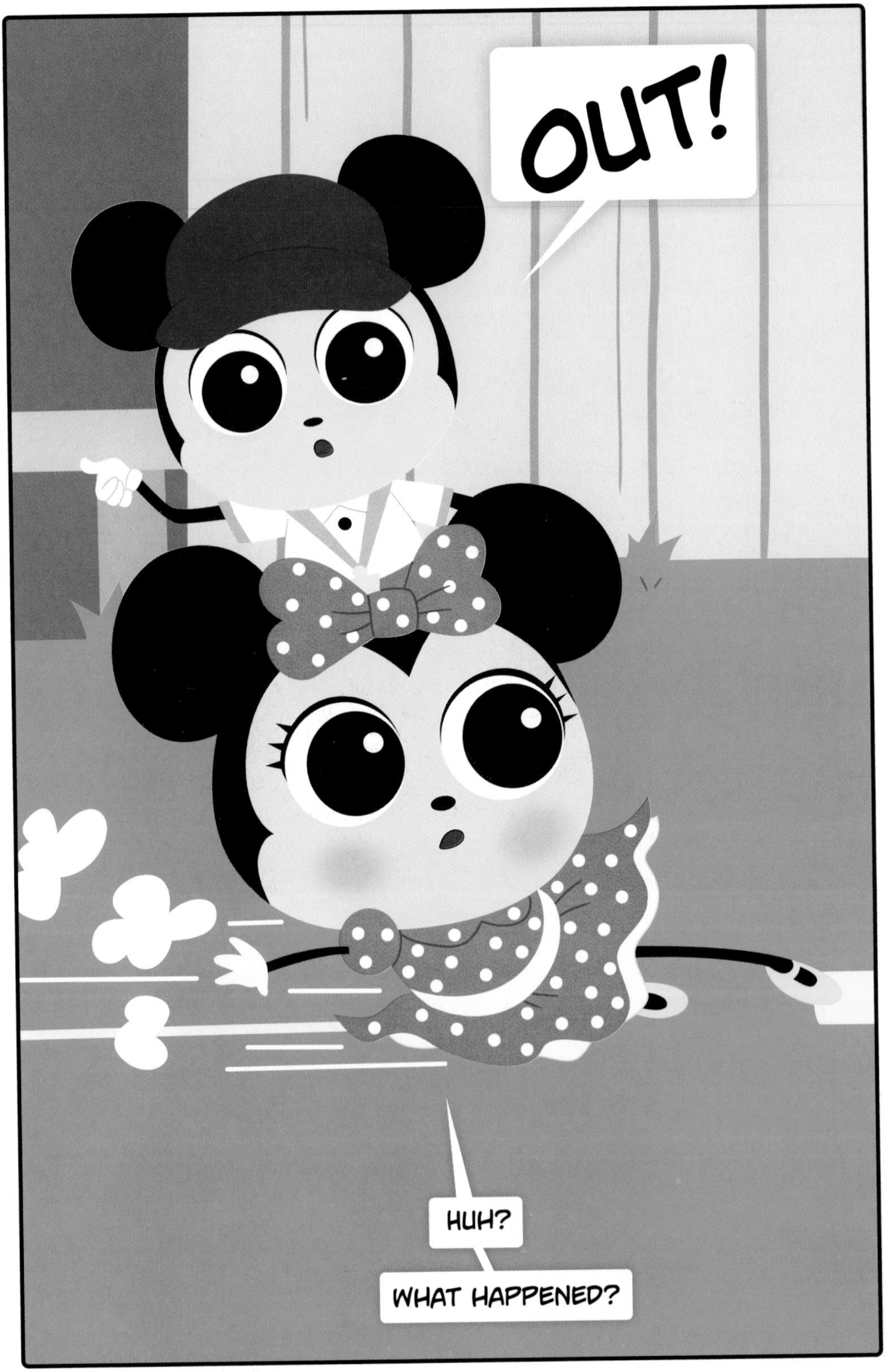
OUT!
HUH?
WHAT HAPPENED?

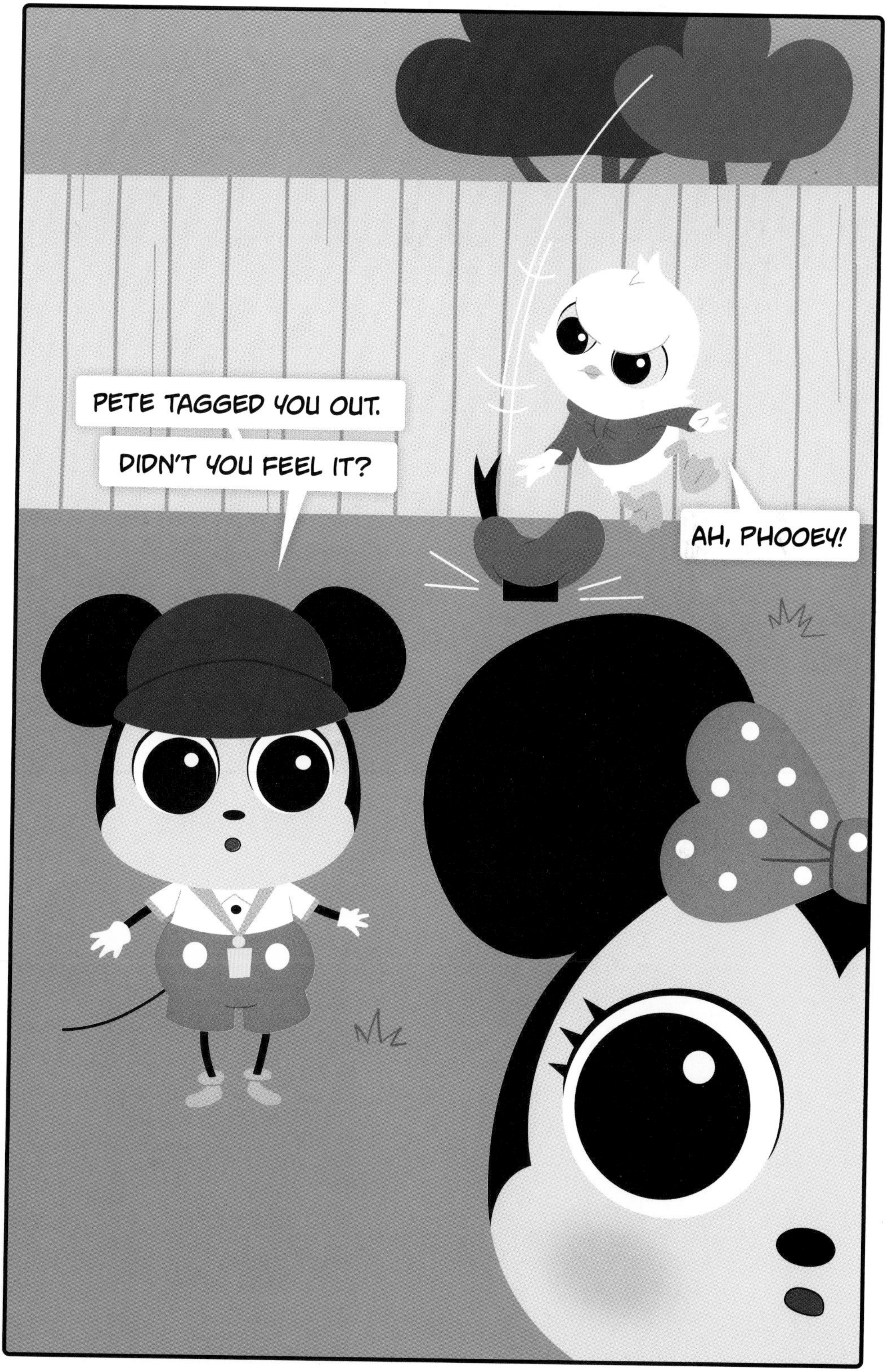
PETE TAGGED YOU OUT.
DIDN'T YOU FEEL IT?
AH, PHOOEY!

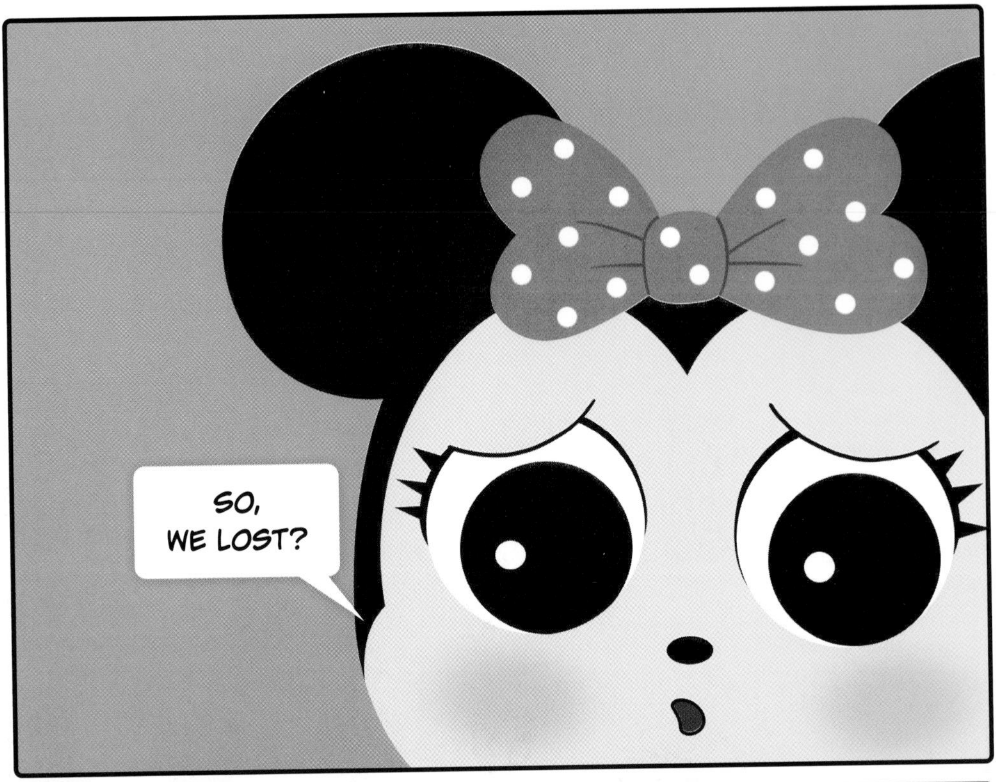
SO, WE LOST?

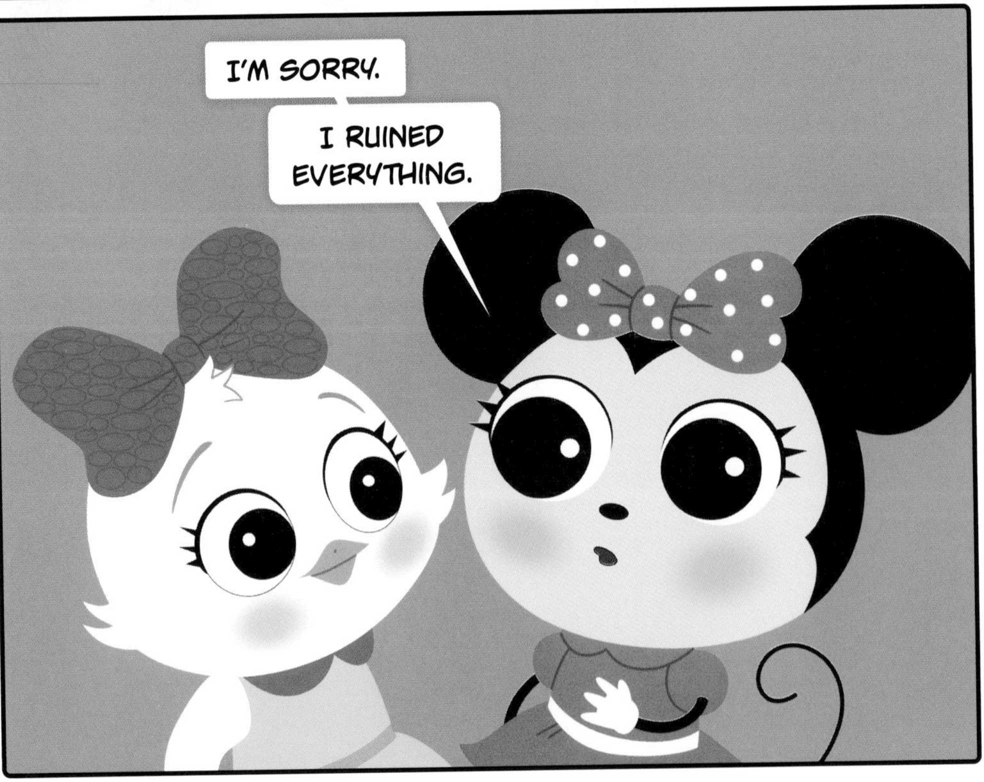
I'M SORRY.
I RUINED EVERYTHING.

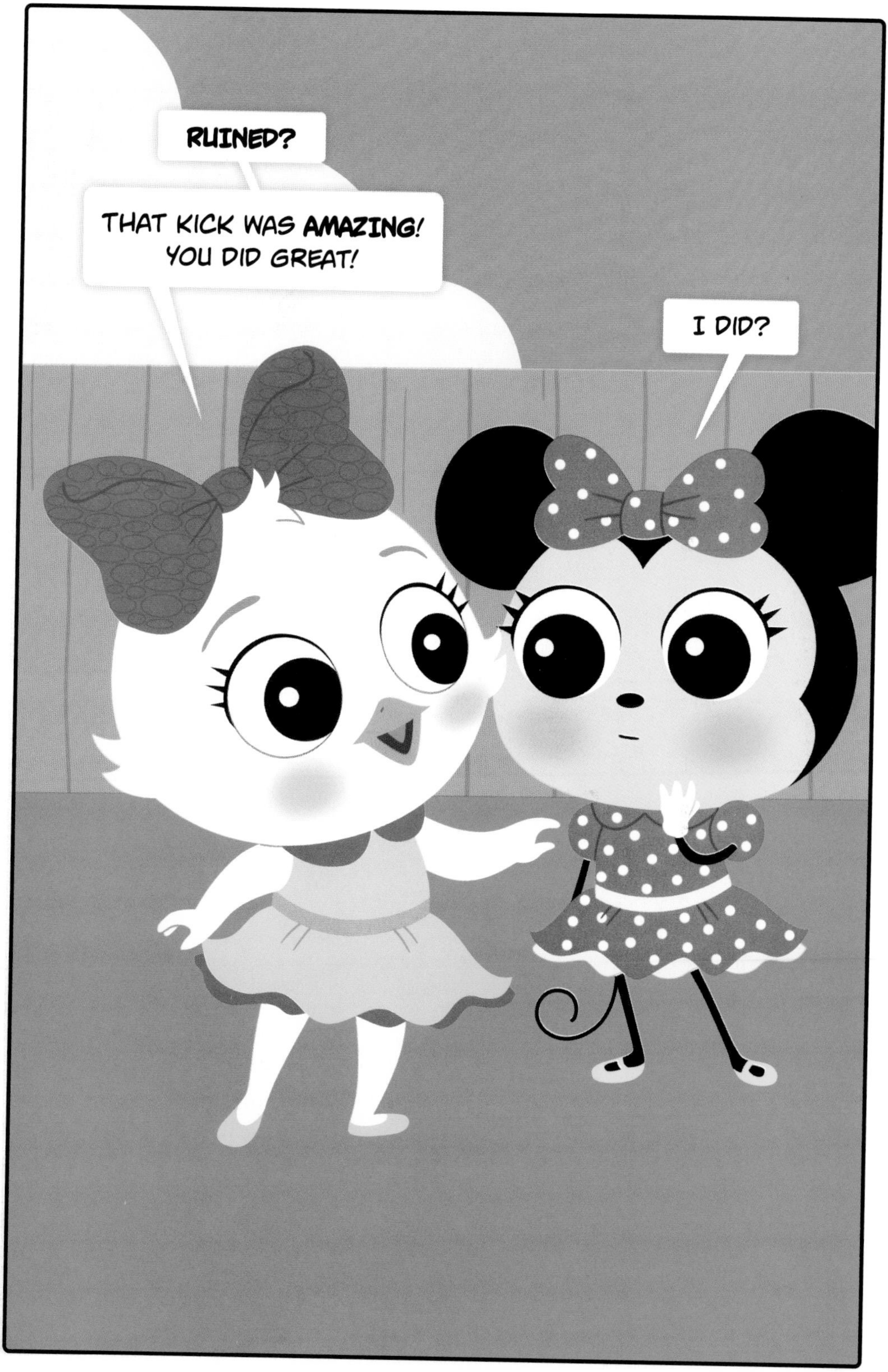
RUINED?
THAT KICK WAS AMAZING! YOU DID GREAT!
I DID?

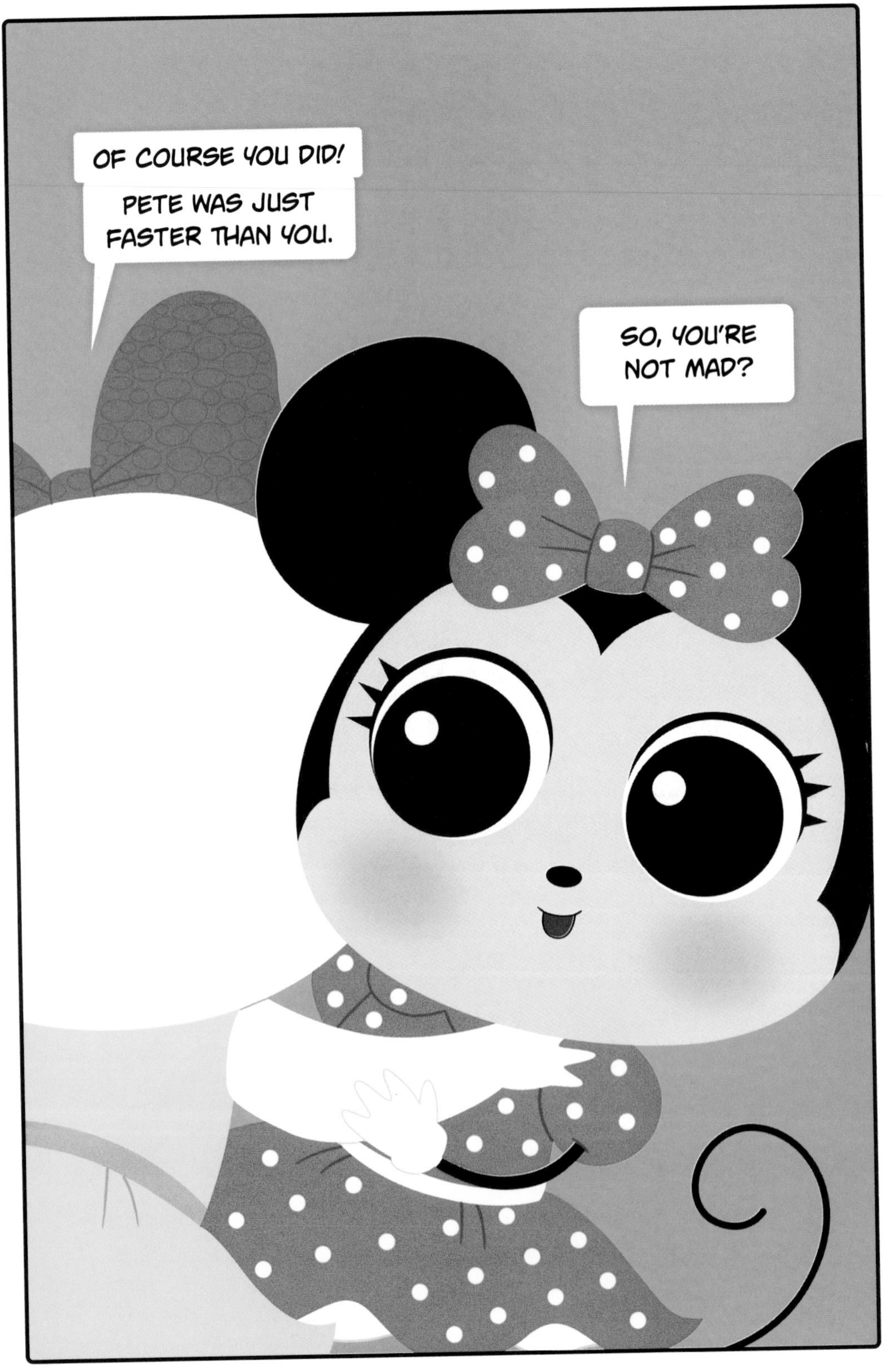
OF COURSE YOU DID!
PETE WAS JUST FASTER THAN YOU.
SO, YOU'RE NOT MAD?

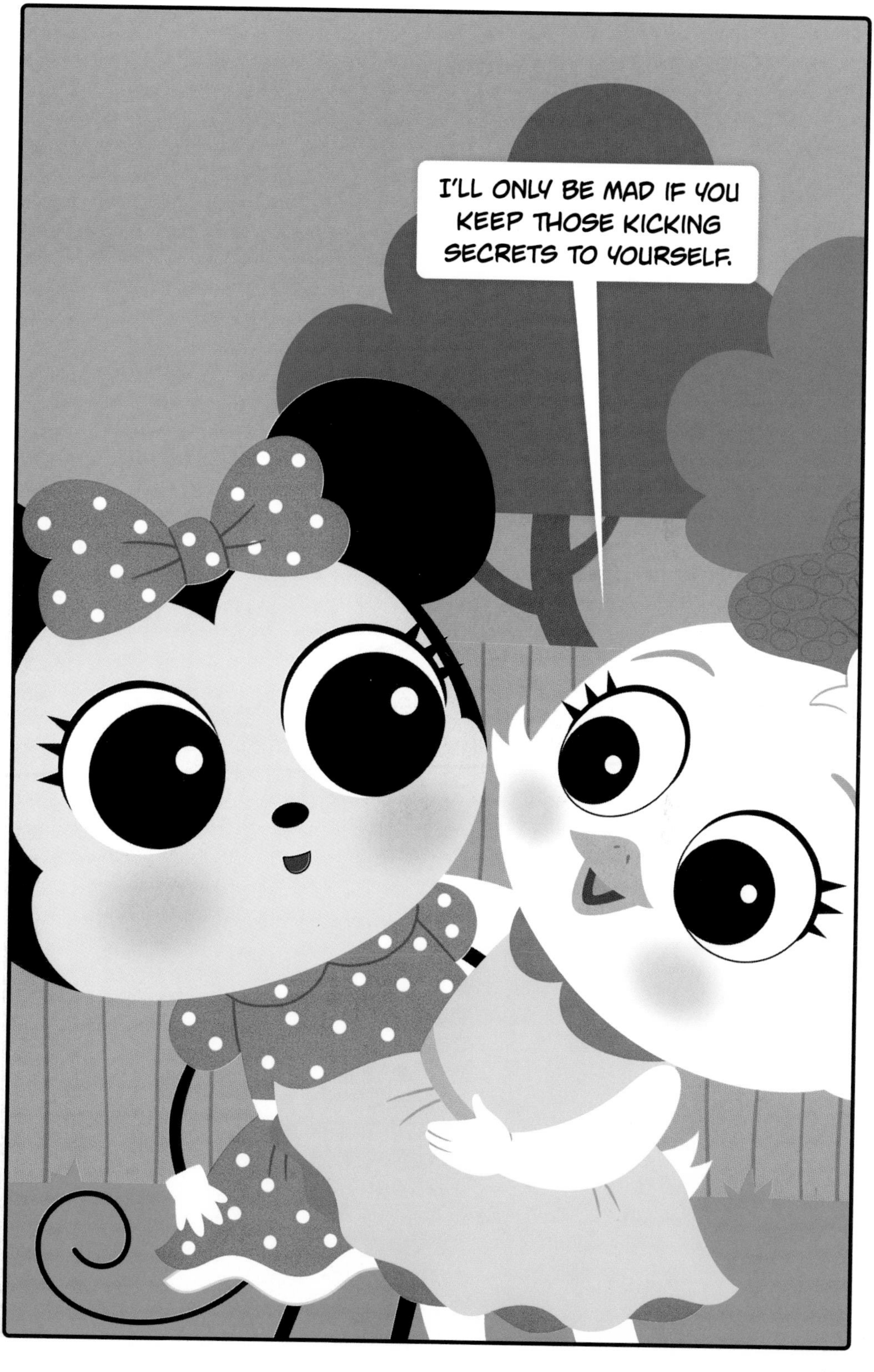
I'LL ONLY BE MAD IF YOU KEEP THOSE KICKING SECRETS TO YOURSELF.

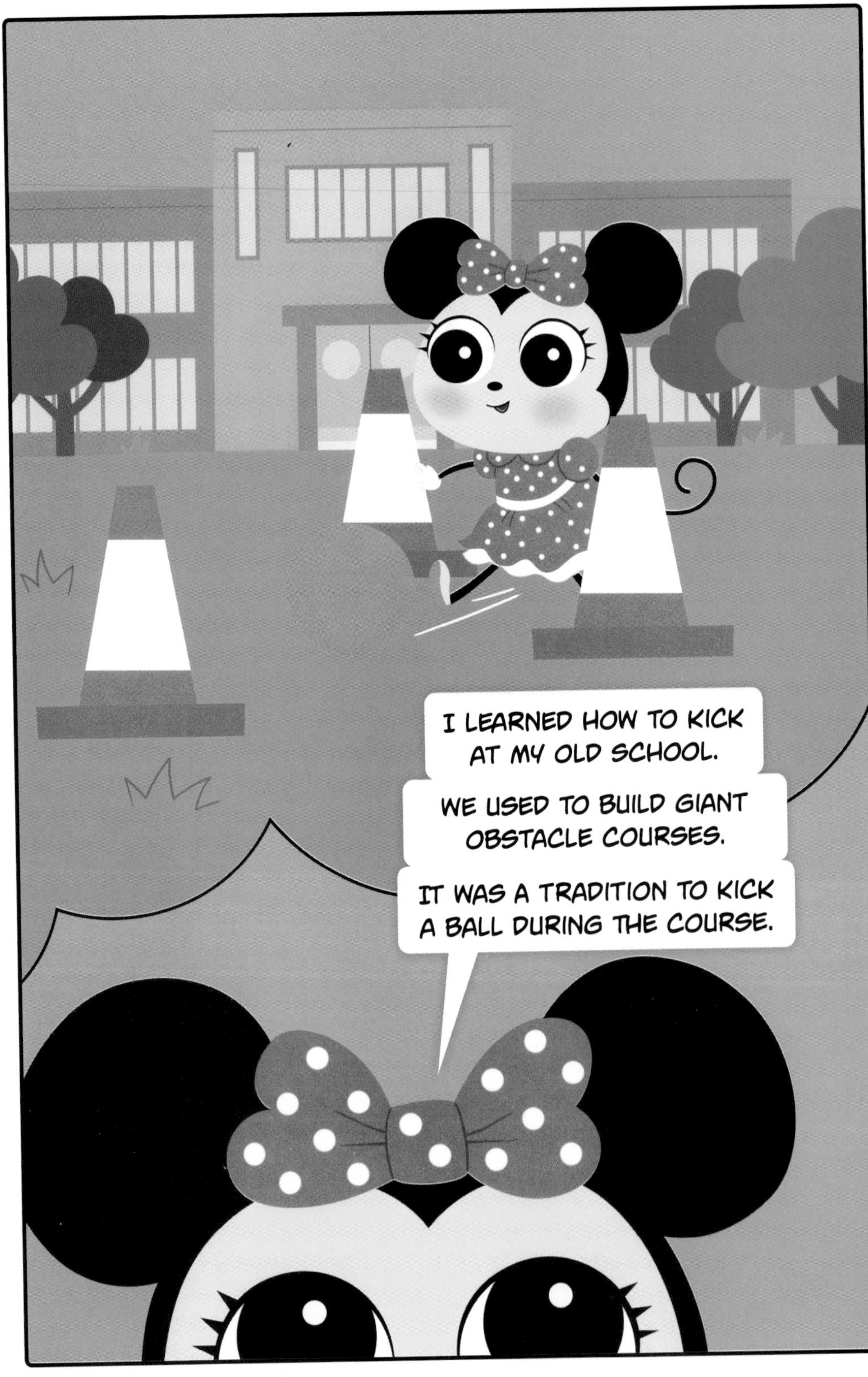
I LEARNED HOW TO KICK AT MY OLD SCHOOL.
WE USED TO BUILD GIANT OBSTACLE COURSES.
IT WAS A TRADITION TO KICK A BALL DURING THE COURSE.

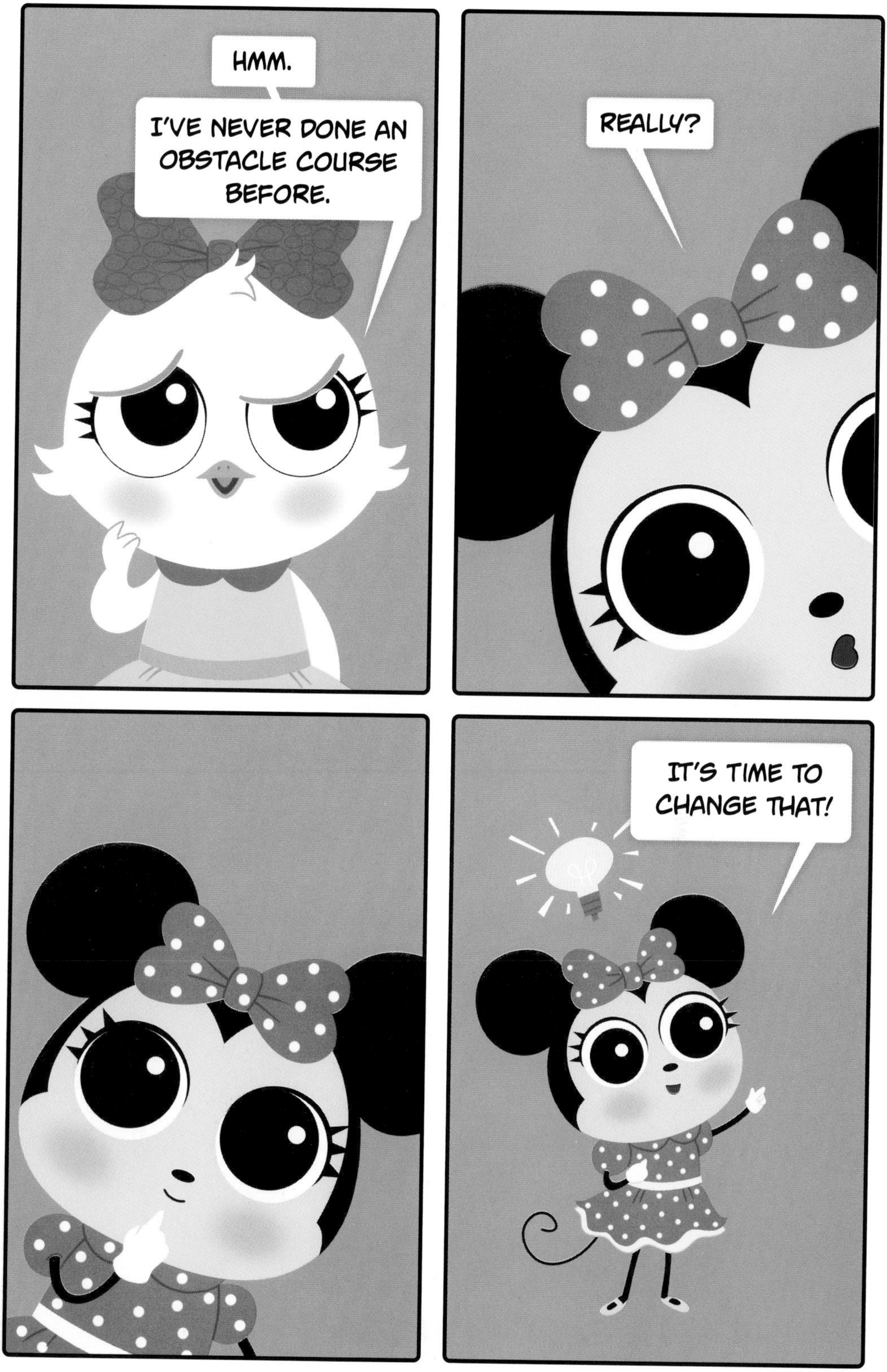
HMM.
I'VE NEVER DONE AN OBSTACLE COURSE BEFORE.
REALLY?
IT'S TIME TO CHANGE THAT!

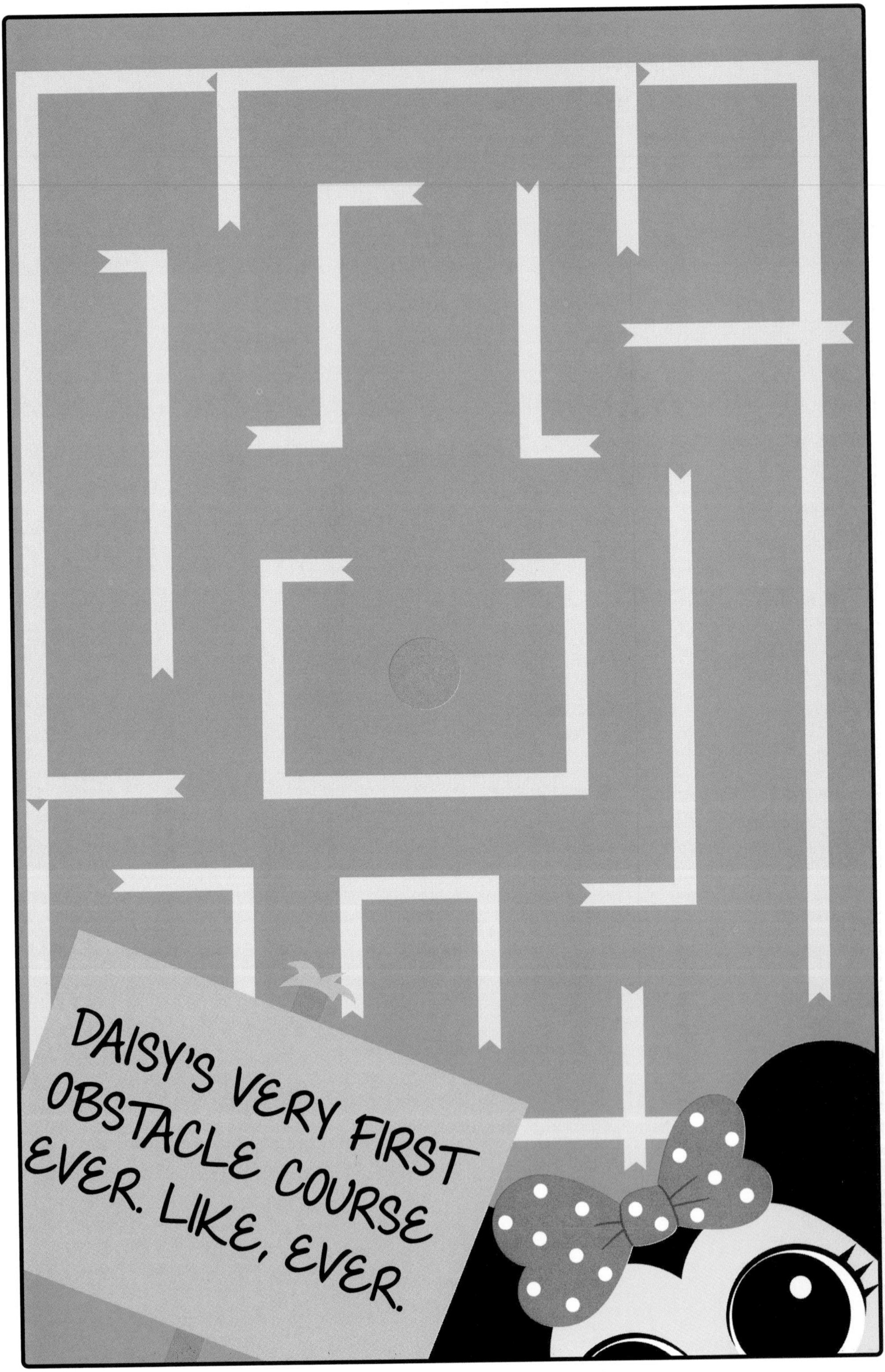
DAISY'S VERY FIRST OBSTACLE COURSE EVER. LIKE, EVER.

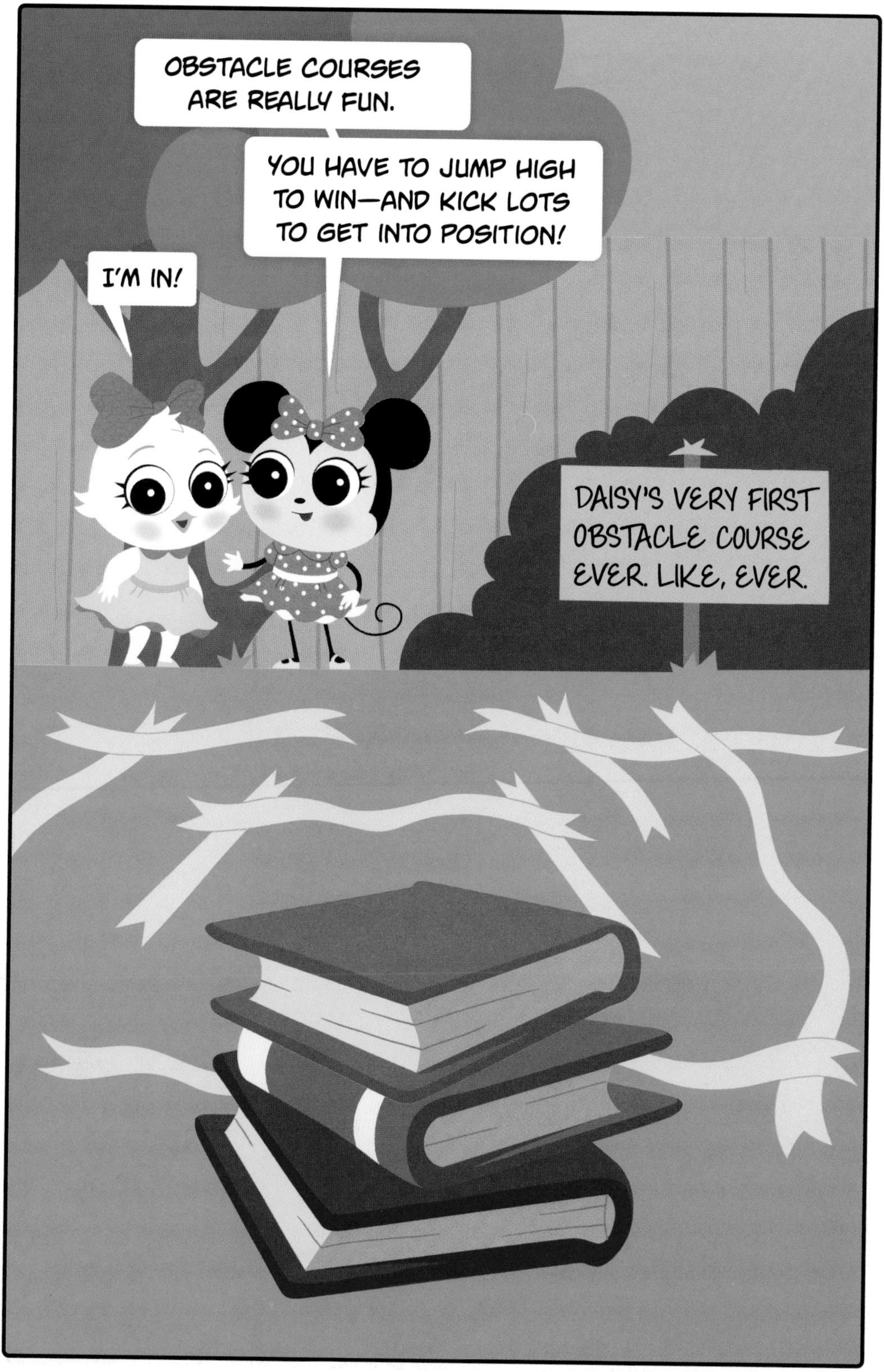
OBSTACLE COURSES ARE REALLY FUN.
YOU HAVE TO JUMP HIGH TO WIN—AND KICK LOTS TO GET INTO POSITION!
I'M IN!
DAISY'S VERY FIRST OBSTACLE COURSE EVER. LIKE, EVER.

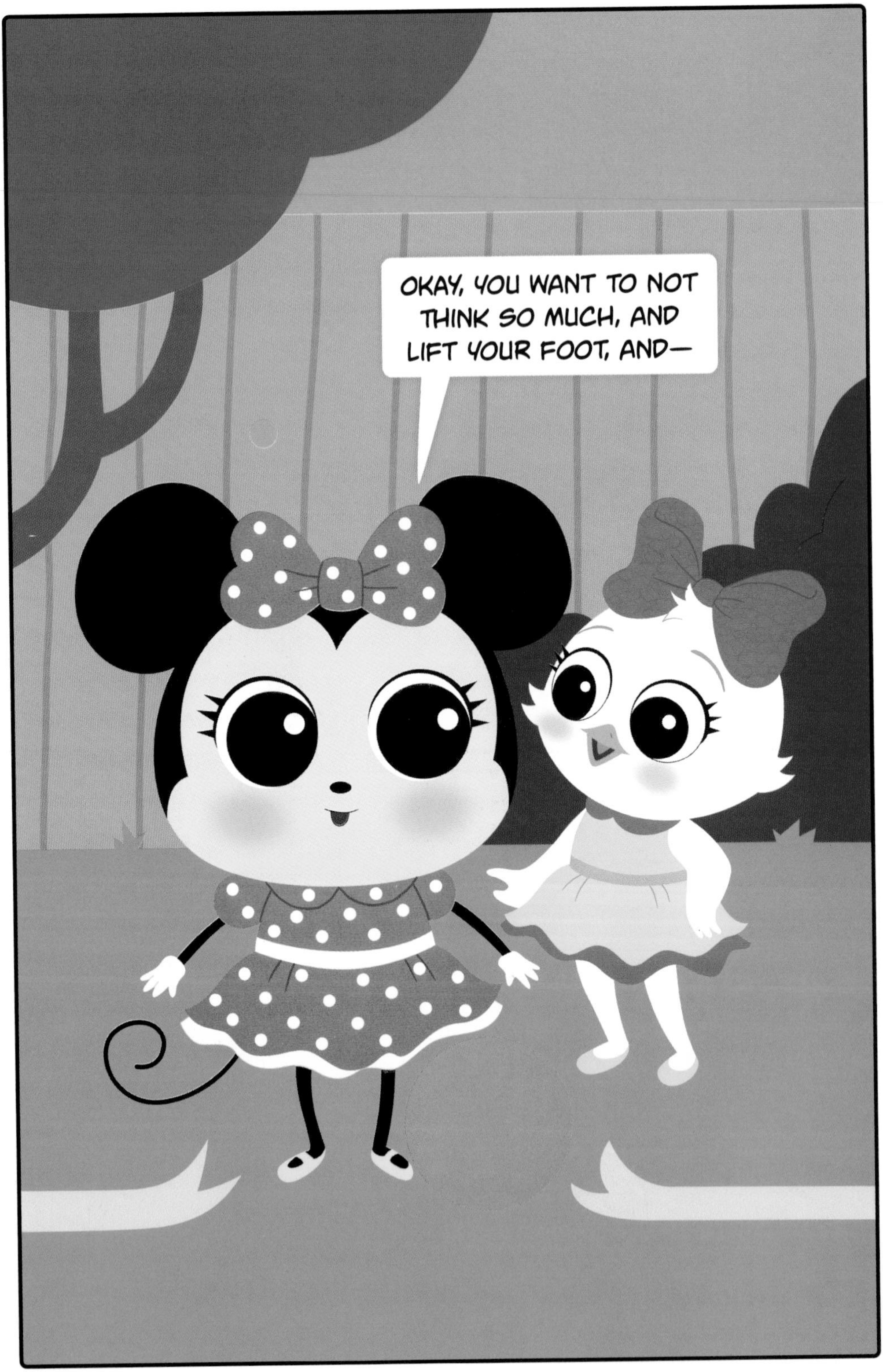
OKAY, YOU WANT TO NOT THINK SO MUCH, AND LIFT YOUR FOOT, AND—

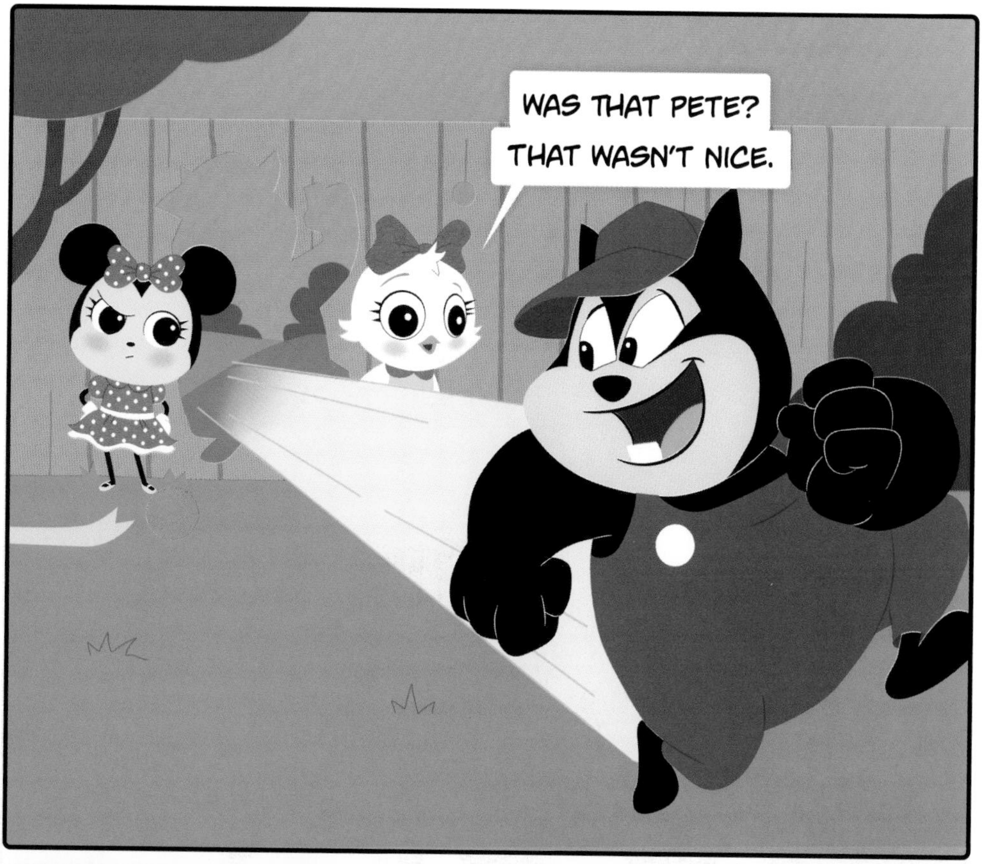
WAS THAT PETE?
THAT WASN'T NICE.

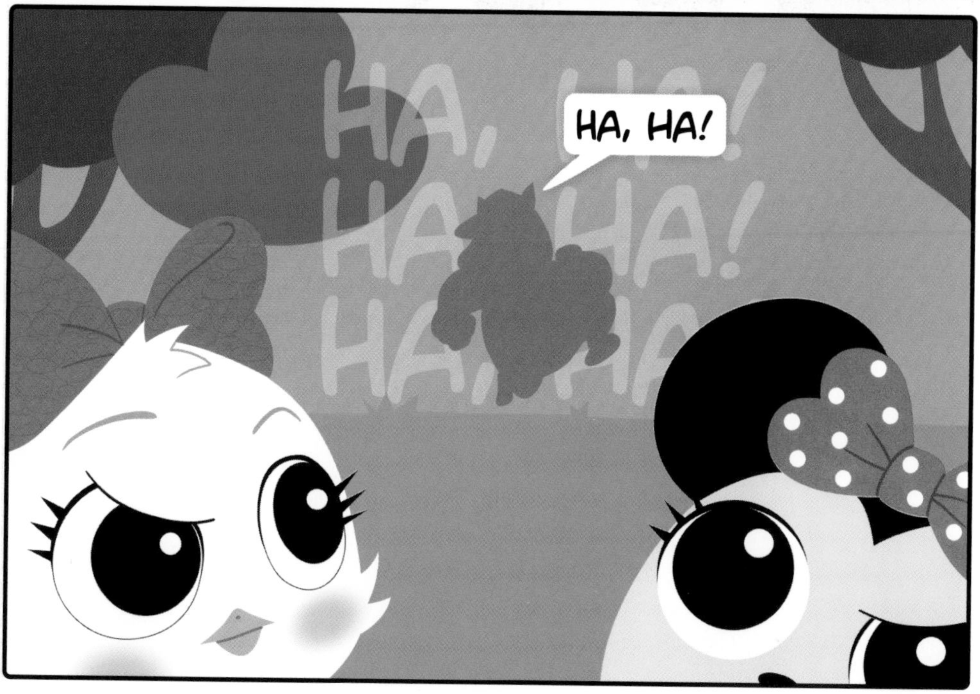
HA, HA!

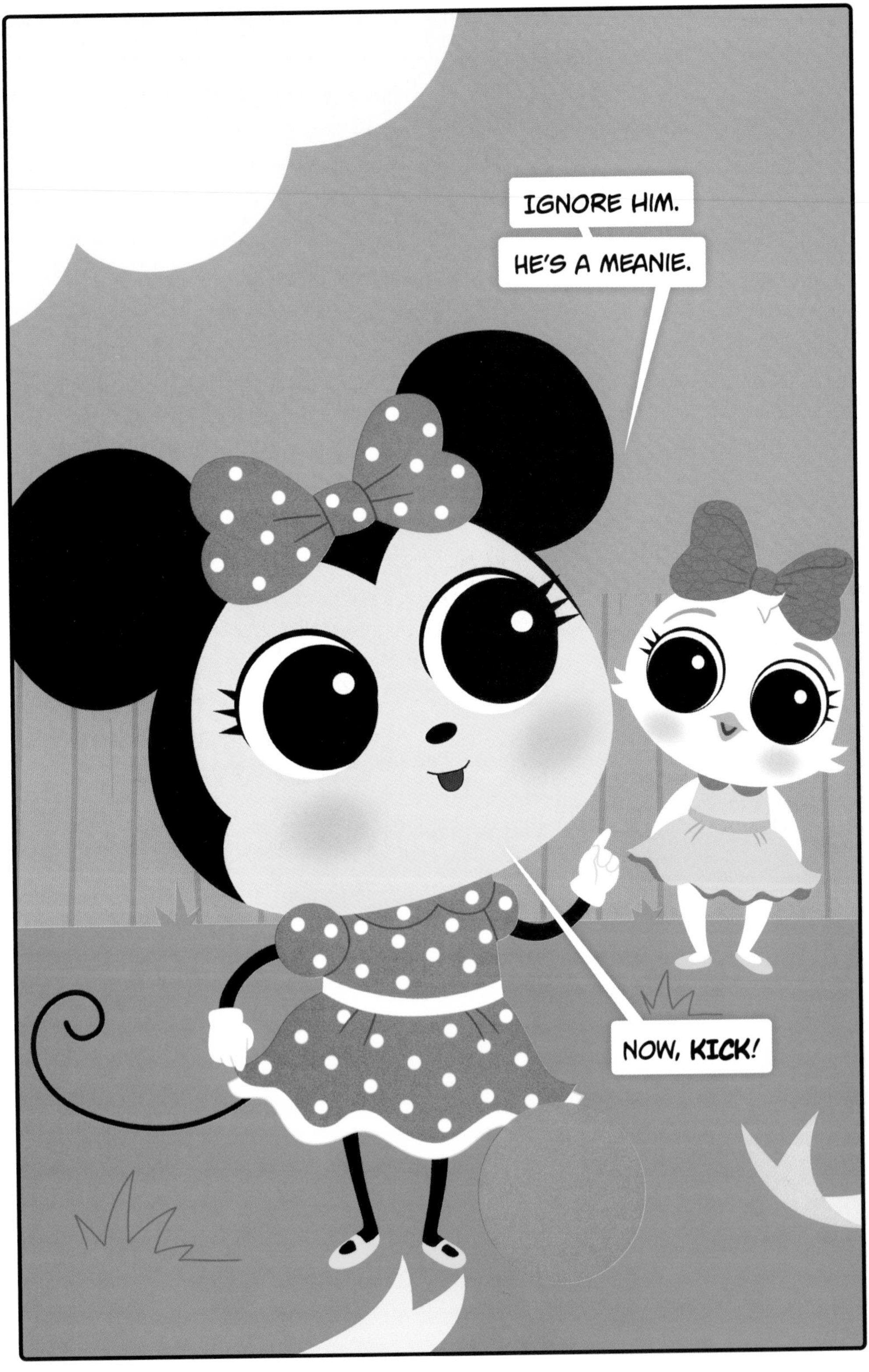
IGNORE HIM.
HE'S A MEANIE.
NOW, KICK!

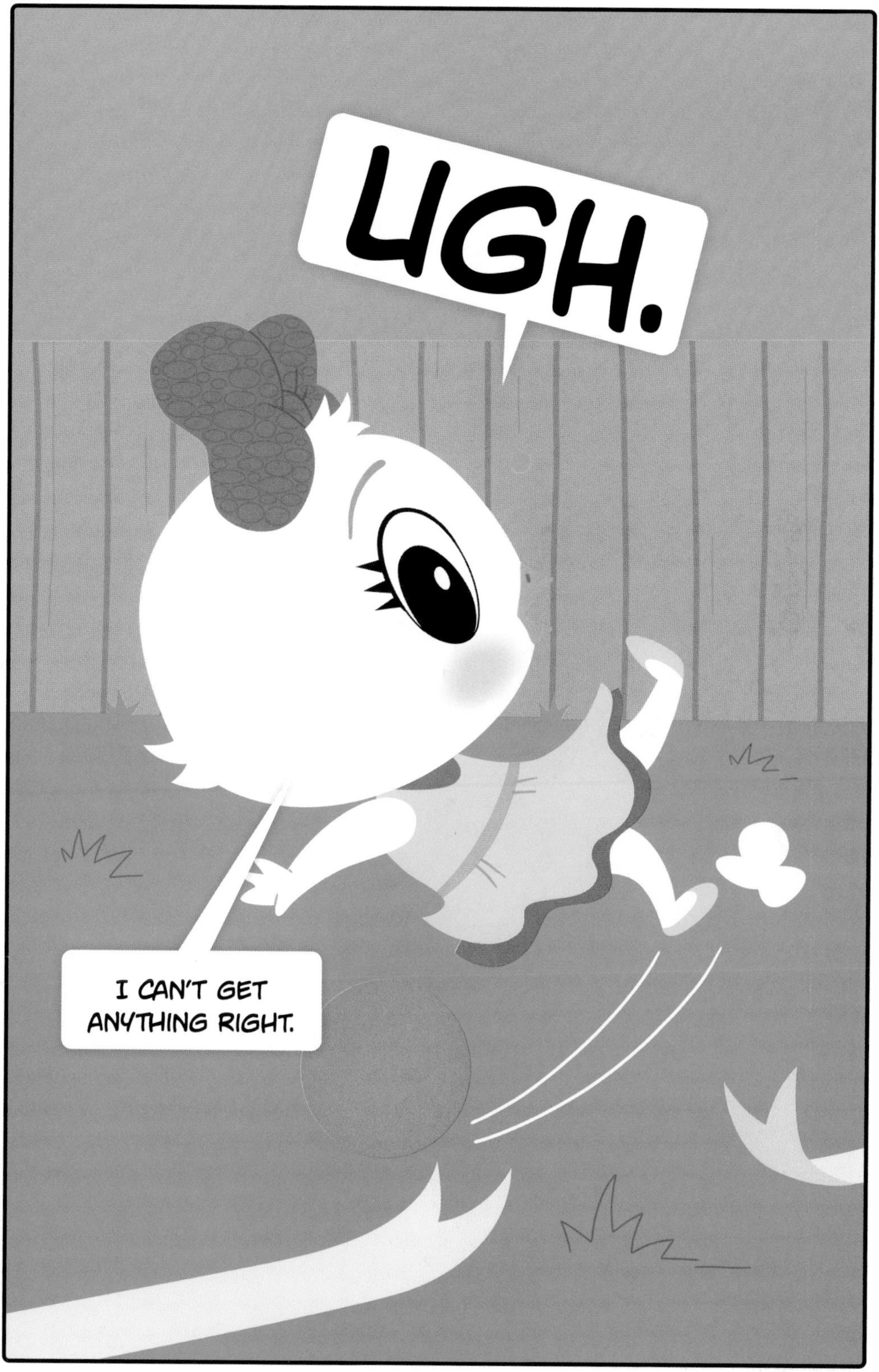
UGH.
I CAN'T GET ANYTHING RIGHT.

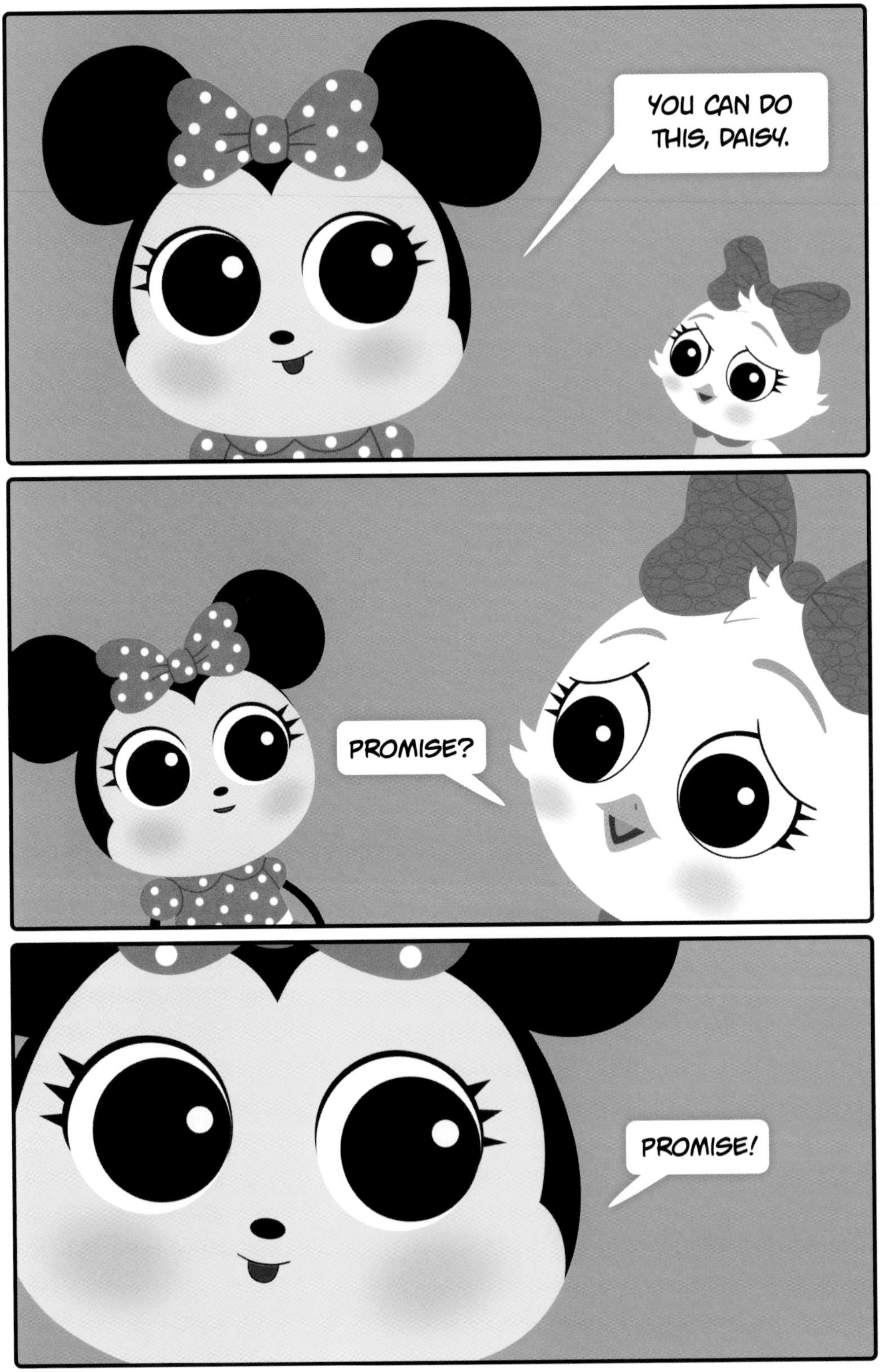
YOU CAN DO THIS, DAISY.
PROMISE?
PROMISE!

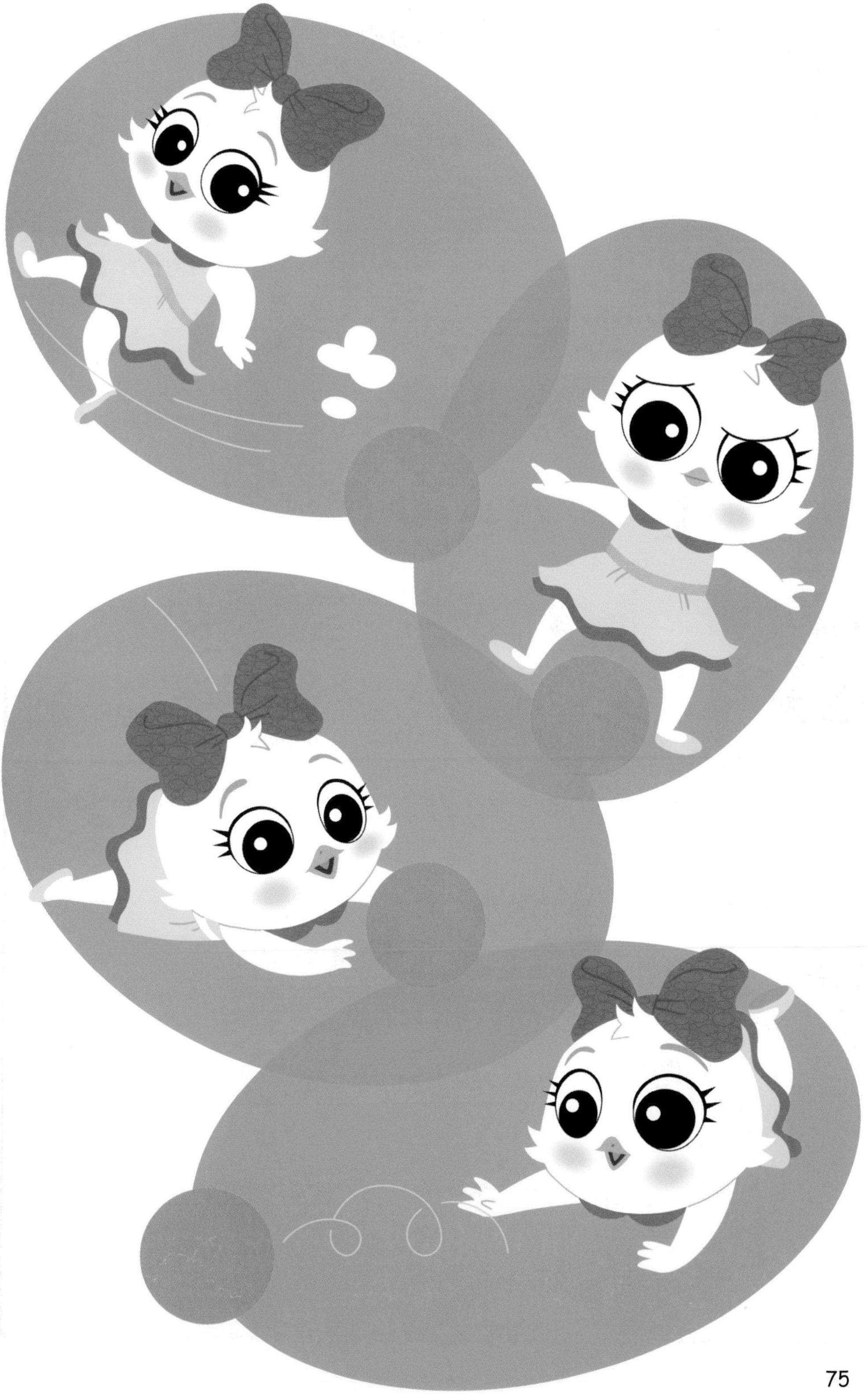

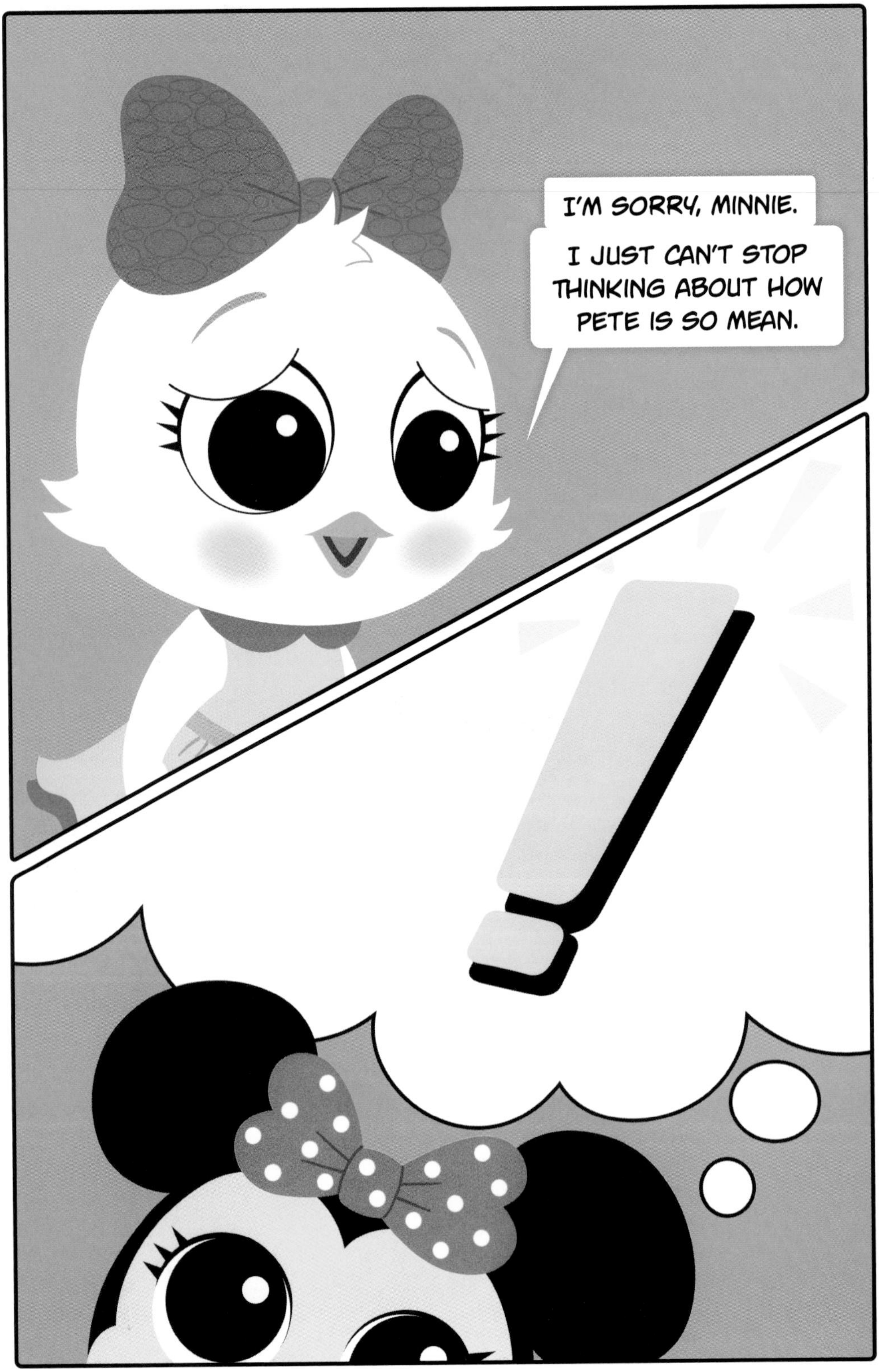
I'M SORRY, MINNIE.
I JUST CAN'T STOP THINKING ABOUT HOW PETE IS SO MEAN.

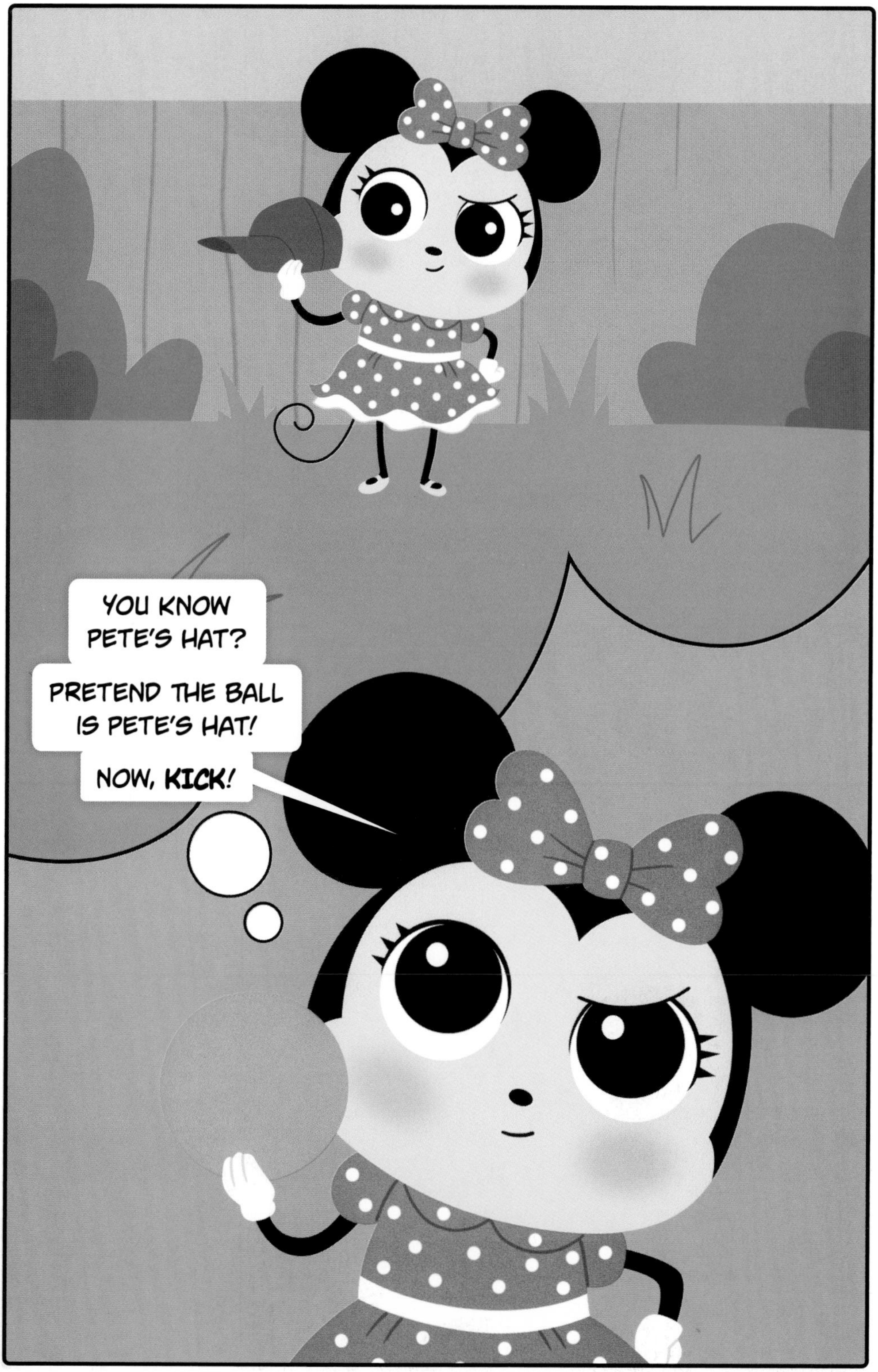
YOU KNOW PETE'S HAT?
PRETEND THE BALL IS PETE'S HAT!
NOW, **KICK**!

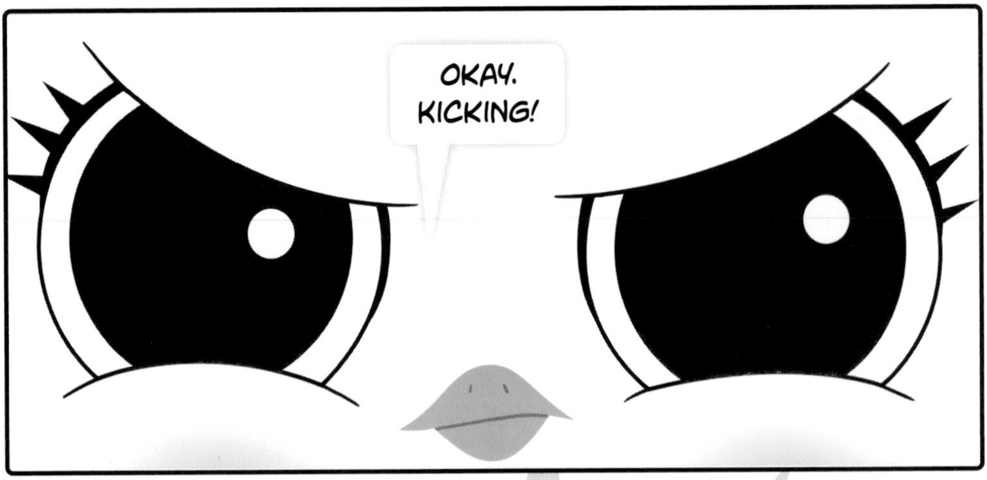
OKAY.
KICKING!

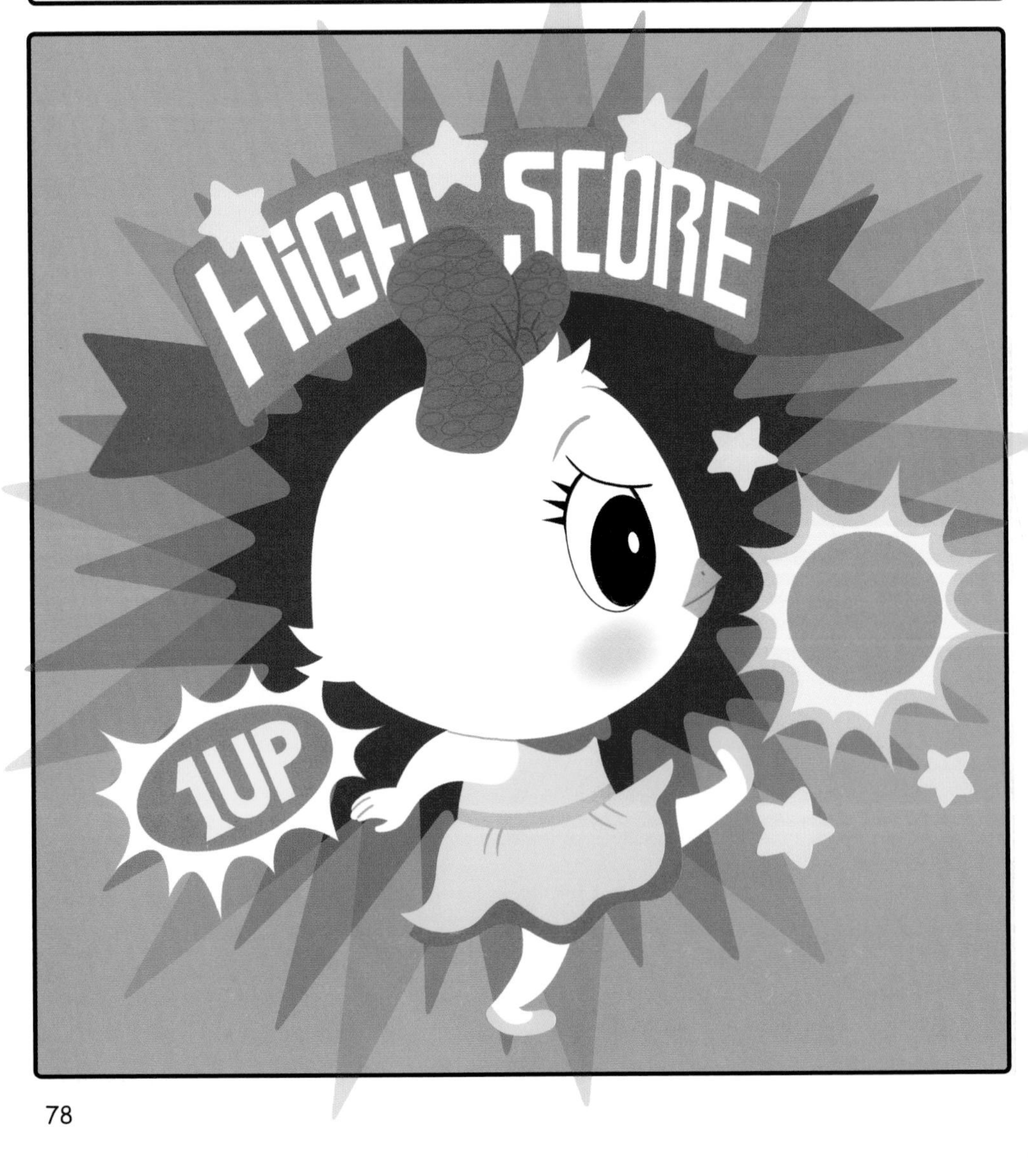
HIGH SCORE
1UP

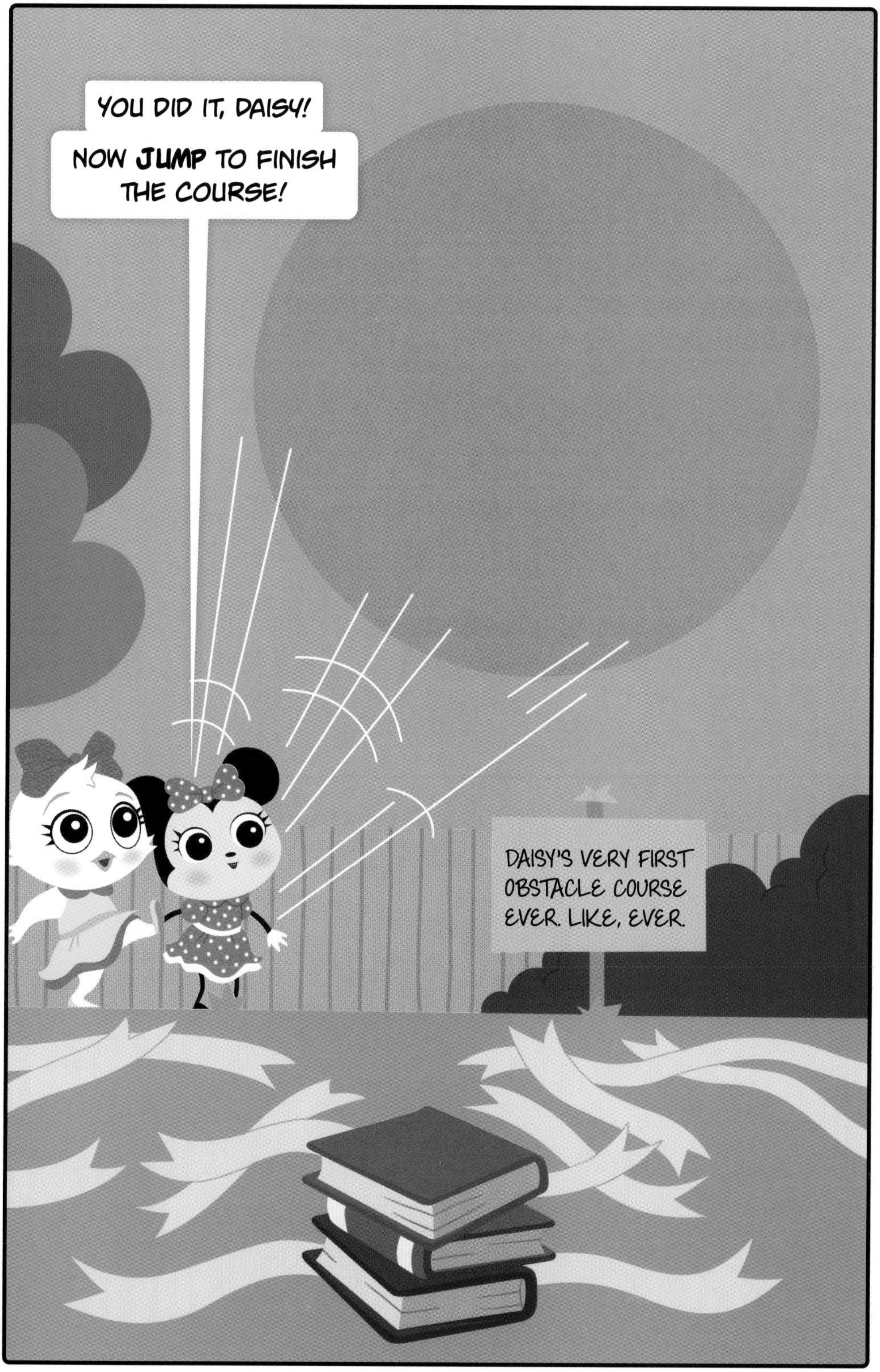
YOU DID IT, DAISY!
NOW JUMP TO FINISH THE COURSE!
DAISY'S VERY FIRST OBSTACLE COURSE EVER. LIKE, EVER.

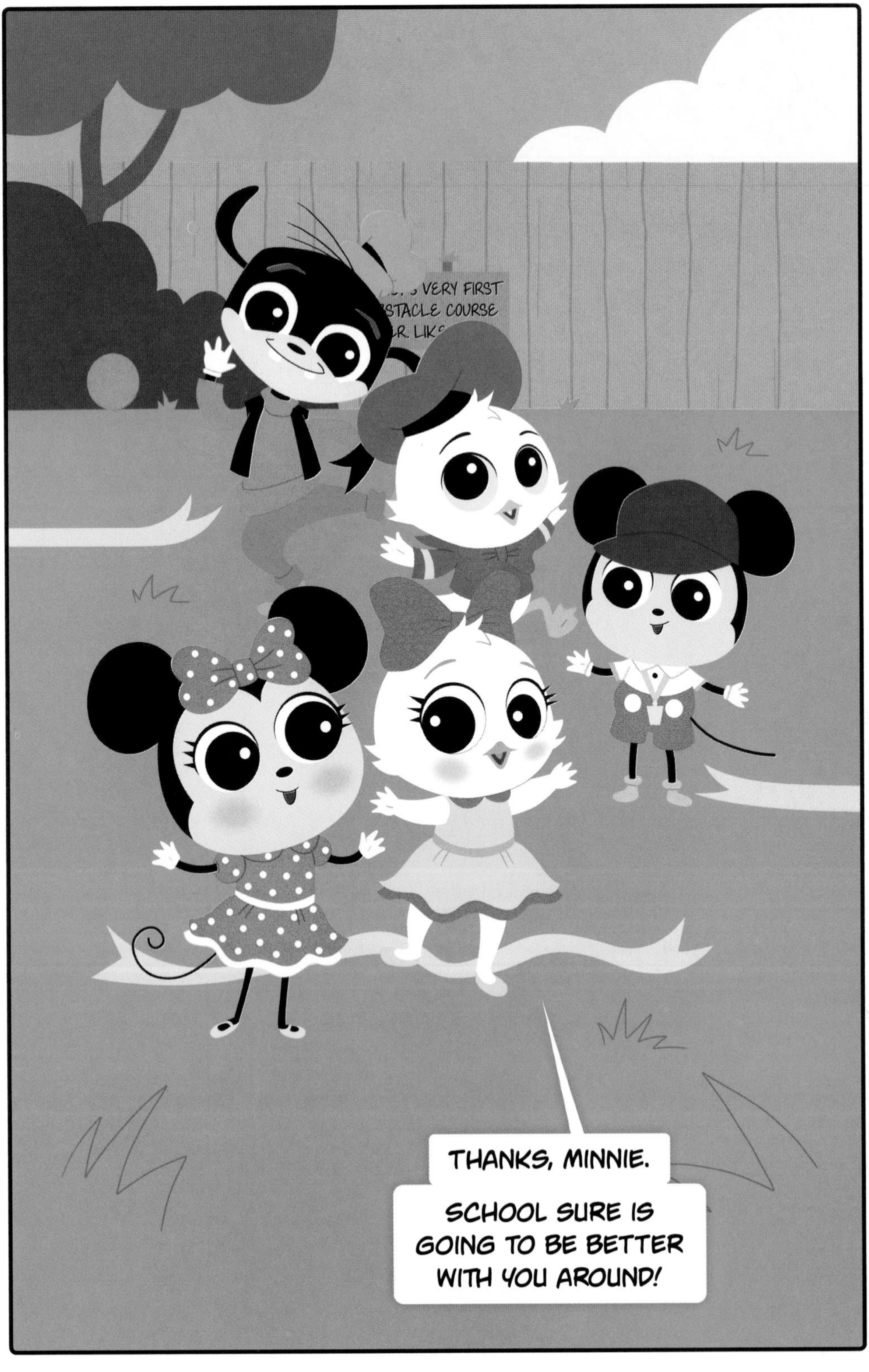
THANKS, MINNIE.
SCHOOL SURE IS GOING TO BE BETTER WITH YOU AROUND!